HIS

NUMBER

ONE

FAN

Danyell A. Wallace

His Number One Fan

His Number One Fan

Copyright©2015 by Danyell A. Wallace
Cover Design by Danyell A. Wallace

His Number One Fan

I Dedicate This Book To
All The Readers Out There!

**

Please be sure to follow me on
Facebook
www.facebook.com/danyellawallace

Twitter and Instagram
@by_Danyell

Other Titles Written by Danyell A. Wallace:
Wanting You
Available in paperback and e-book on
Amazon.
Amazon.com/author/danyellawallace

His Number One Fan

one
Nyla

I'm standing in my living room looking at all the pieces of my luggage that I have scattered on the floor. *Did I pack too much? I'm only going to be gone for two weeks. I guess that's what I get for having too many clothes to choose from. Plus, I didn't have any clue to what Caleb had planned for us so I guess I should be safe than sorry.*

I grab my cellphone off the coffee table and I look at the time. It was three o'clock in the morning, and I had exactly ten minutes to make sure I had everything packed and ready to go, before heading downstairs to catch my taxi to the airport.

Quietly I walk around my apartment that I was currently sharing with my friend Jordyn, making sure I wasn't forgetting anything. I walk down the hall towards my room when I hear a door open from behind me. I turn around and see a guy I didn't even know, sneaking out Jordyn's room. The hallway was dark, so I couldn't make out what he looked like, but from the light that was shining from the living room into the hallway, I could tell he was half dressed, and wearing only a pair of jeans. He was carrying his shirt and shoes in one hand, tip toeing the rest of the way down the hall and into the living room.

I stand in the hallway, not saying a word, watching him until he disappears around the corner. As soon as the front door shuts, I turn around and continue walking down the hall, and into my room.

With the lights already on in my room, I quickly look around making sure I had everything I needed. With nothing else to get, I grab my purse off my bed and I look inside to make sure I had my flight itinerary and driver's license. I cut my lights off and close my door behind me and I make my way back to living room, where I find Jordyn curled up on the love seat looking at me.

She had on her oversized East NYU sweatshirt and a pair of boxer shorts. Her curls were pulled away from her face and up into a bun. Her brown skin was clear of makeup, and she was wearing a pair of prescription glasses that were hiding her sleepy eyes.

"Jordyn what are you doing up so early? Did I wake you?"

"Naw that jackass that decided to leave without saying goodbye woke me up." She says with a yawn. "Are you packed and ready to go?"

"Looks like it." I respond while throwing my carry-on bag across my shoulder, then I grab my other pieces of luggage and I walk to the door, placing them beside it.

"Well I guess I'll see you in two weeks." I say with a smile on my face.

"I'm going to miss you Nyla." Jordyn says in a fake whiny voice.

"Girl please. You know you're going to enjoy having this place to yourself."

"You're right." She says laughing.

She gets off the love seat and walks over and gives me hug.

"Make sure you call or text me when your plane lands in California."

"I will."

"Here let me help you with your bags."

We grab my bags and walk out the door, and take the elevator down. When we make it to the lobby, she helps me wheel my bags outside where we find my taxi parked, and waiting on me. The driver steps out and takes all of my bags and loads them into the trunk of the taxi.

"Thanks Jordyn."

"No problem. Have a safe trip!"

"You know I will." I say getting into the already open door of the cab. With a final wave, I close the door behind me.

The ride to the JFK Airport was pretty peaceful, considering that New York traffic is usually busy and crazy. But I guess since it was close to four in the morning, everyone was still asleep.

I pull out my cellphone and I quickly send Caleb a text letting him know that I was heading to the airport, even though I knew it was one in the morning his time. Knowing him, he probably had his phone on silent anyway.

Before I could put my phone away, a text comes through from Caleb saying that he couldn't wait to see me and to have a safe trip. It has been four and half years since I last saw him. Even though we talked, texted, and occasionally skyped each other practically every day. I was really looking forward to seeing my best friend. Smiling to myself I put my phone away and I relax and enjoy the rest of the ride to the airport.

* * *

I make it to the airport earlier than expected. As soon as I had my bags unloaded I make my way inside and straight to the Southern East Airline Express check in area. After verifying my info through the system, I check in all my bags and I almost pass out when I see how much it was going to cost me. *Next time I will have to travel light.* I swipe my credit card and I wait on my boarding passes and receipts to print from the kiosk. Then I stand in line with all my luggage waiting to check them at the counter with the airport attendant.

When my name is called I place my luggage one at a time on the scale. The attendant verifies that I am in fact Nyla Freeman and that I was traveling to Houston, Texas then to Sacramento, California.

I take the escalator to the next level where I go through airport security with no problems, then I grab a cup of coffee at one of the fast food restaurants. With thirty minutes left until I was scheduled to board, I find my gate and I take a seat until it's time for the attendant to call for boarding.

I pull out my phone to turn it on airplane mode, when

I see another text from Caleb wanting to confirm when I was scheduled to land in Sacramento, so I quickly text a reply.

Nyla: Why are you up?

Caleb: Excited to see you. I feel like a kid on Christmas Eve.

Nyla: Whatever. What are you doing?

Caleb: Working on some lyrics with Mason. Have you listened to the tracks I put on the MP3 I sent you?

Nyla: Not yet, I will during the flight.

Caleb: Cool.

Good morning and thank you for choosing Southern East Airline. We're going to go ahead and start boarding zone one. Thank you.

I hear over the intercom.

Nyla: Hey gotta go. Getting ready to board.

Caleb: C u soon.

I put my phone away, and I grab my carry-on and

purse, then I get in line.

As soon as I board, I place my carry-on in the above bin then I take my seat near the window. I pull out my MP3 and I stick my earphones in my ears, then I press play.

With my seat belt secured, I lean my head against the headrest listening to the hypnotic sound of Caleb's guitar and the soothing voice of Wildfire's lead singer, that I have yet to meet, Mason Scott, coming through my earphones.

They were both very talented from what I was listening to, and I couldn't wait to hear them and the rest of the members of Wildfire play live.

About a year ago Caleb's dad, Isaac Walker and his manager Richie aka Rich, was very impressed with Wildfire when they saw them playing at The Grind, a club they've been playing at for two years. They were so impressed that his dad asked them to come on tour with them. So in a couple of weeks Wildfire will be on tour, opening up for his dad's band, Hurricane.

I was so lost in the music that I didn't even realize that another passenger had sat beside me, until they accidentally bumped my arm with theirs. After accepting their apology, I look around the plane and see it's filled with passengers already settled in their seats. The flight attendant walks forward and stops in the middle of the aisle and starts going over the emergency and safety procedures. I've been up since two o'clock this morning, and the coffee I had earlier wasn't helping. My eyes remained focused on the attendant, until they just couldn't stay open any longer. The sound of Mason's voice was still playing in my ear like a lullaby, and eventually I fall into a peaceful sleep.

two
Caleb

"Yo Caleb!"

"Yo!" I respond back, then I continue to strum a couple of chords on my guitar.

I stop briefly when Evan, my roommate and also the rhythm guitarist of our band stops in my doorway with a cute brunette that I've seen around the club trying to get the attention from all the members of our band, standing there topless in a pair of panties.

"Hey Caleb." She speaks to me from what I guess she thought was a sexy tone.

"Sup." I respond, tearing my gaze away from her and back to my music.

"Evan and I wanted to know if you wanted to have some fun?"

Damn her voice was getting on my nerves.

Shaking my head to myself I respond. "No I'm alright."

"See Jess I told you he doesn't get down like that." Evan speaks up.

"That's too bad, because I've been told I give the best blow jobs." She says as if I'm going to change my mind.

"I know baby, but he doesn't want to play right now."

Pissed about the whole scene going on, I turn my attention back to the both of them.

"What the fuck do you want?" I ask directing my attention to Evan.

"Dude! Shit I'm sorry for bothering you. I actually wanted to know what time you were going to pick up... What's her name?"

I take a deep breath to calm my nerves.

"Her name is Nyla, and her flight is supposed to be here at 6 tonight."

"Well it's fifteen after five. You know how traffic can be on a Friday. Especially when everyone is getting off work trying to get home."

"I know. I'm just trying to get these lyrics on paper, for the song that I'm working on with Mason."

"He has a girlfriend?" I hear Jess ask Evan.

"Naw. They've been best friends since the fourth grade." He responds.

"Oh okay." She responds, sounding hopeful.

"Fine man, I'll leave you alone." Evan says. "But if I were you, I would leave now before she thinks you forgot about her."

"Shit, maybe you're right. Alright I'm going. Do you need anything while I'm out?"

"Naw I have everything I need right here." He says pulling Jess's body closer to his. "I'll try to remember to use my manners and keep it down. I don't want Nyla thinking I'm a freak."

"Whatever man. I'm out."

I remove the acoustic guitar strap from around my neck, and I place the guitar back on its stand, and I grab the keys to my Camaro off my dresser. Evan steps aside, while Jess stays put in the door way, not leaving much room. I roll my eyes, and walk past her. She leans forward, causing her body to rub against mine.

"Bye Caleb." She yells down the hall.

"Fuckin' groupie." I say under my breath before walking out the front door.

* * *

"Shit!" I say for the hundredth time that night while hitting the steering wheel. Traffic was ridiculous. I look at the time on my LCD screen and see it's now 6:35pm. I was officially late. I grab my cellphone off the passenger seat and I dial Nyla's number again, but it goes straight to voice mail, so I leave a message.

"Nyla. Hey it's me. I just wanted to let you know that I'm stuck in traffic. Trust me I didn't forget about you. Please call me when you get this message. Bye."

I end the call and look straight ahead, waiting on traffic to start moving again. Minutes later, traffic still hasn't budged.

I rest my head against the headrest and my mind wonders back to the first time I met Nyla, in the fourth grade. It was around the time she and her family had just moved to California from Texas. Her dad was an Officer in the Air Force, so that was the main reason for their move here.

He was stationed at Beale Air Force Base, so instead of living in base housing, her dad decided they would buy a house in Sacramento, California; which was only an hour or so from Beale AFB.

They ended up buying a house, two houses down from mine. I remember that day as if it was yesterday. I was riding my bike past their house when I saw Nyla sitting in her yard on a blanket playing with her dolls, while her mom, dad, and the movers unloaded the moving truck.

She was this skinny girl with long frizzy curly hair, and she wore these big ass glasses that were too big for her face.

I rode my bike past her house several times that day because I was so curious about the new girl on my street. When she finally looked up in my direction, it caught me by surprise. I wasn't paying attention when my bike hit the curb throwing me off my bike. I flew face first onto the sidewalk skinning up my chin, elbows, and knees. I looked up at her from my position on the ground and saw her still staring at me. I was in so much pain that I didn't want her to see me cry so I got up and hopped back on my bike and rode home, and boy did I cry as soon as I put my kick stand down to park my bike.

Two days after my bike accident, I finally found the courage to talk to her, on her first day of school. Since she started school in the middle of the year, in the beginning it was hard for her to make friends. We didn't have the same teacher, but we shared the same lunch period. Being the good boy that my parents raised me to be, I got up from the lunch table I usually sat eating with my group of friends, and I walked over and introduced myself to her. At first she just stared at me. I stood there watching her looking me over. Her eyes eventually landed on the stitches on my chin that I ended up having to get.

"Are you that boy that flipped over his bike?" She asked me.

"Um yeah." I responded.

She smiled up at me then started laughing.

"My name is Nyla Freeman. What's your name?"

"Caleb. Caleb Walker."

"Well Caleb, would you like to sit down with me?" She asked, hoping and praying I would say yes.

Without saying a word, I pulled out a chair and sat down, and from that day on we became the best of friends.

Every day after school we walked home together. My mom was a stay at home mom, while my dad was on a so called road tour with his band, Hurricane. Nyla would come by my house after school when her parents were still at work. Her dad was out of town a lot on military business, and her mom was an ER Nurse that caused her to be away from home for a long period of time due to her crazy work hours at the hospital. So Nyla would spend most of her afternoons and nights at my house.

By the time we reached junior high, we practically acted like brother and sister. The only difference was I was white and she was black. I have straight dirty blond hair and she had long brown curly hair. My eyes are green and hers are light brown. No one attempted to try and tell us that we couldn't be siblings because of our differences. Even if they did, we didn't care. We had other friends, but Nyla and I were close and no one could break that. Even our parents became close friends to a point that my parents looked at Nyla as if she was a part of the family, and the same went with Nyla's family. I was the son they never had.

The summer before our junior year of high school was to begin was probably one of the worst days of both of our lives. I remember sitting in my bedroom late one night watching tv when Nyla came knocking on my window. As soon as I looked out the window and saw her tear streaked face, I knew something was wrong. I helped her inside and she didn't hesitate and told me that her dad was being transferred to another military base in Germany.

The thought of going through the rest of high school without each other was indescribable. Even though it was tough we kept in contact with each other and promised each other that we would see each other again. Four and a half years later, that promise was finally being honored.

Instead of spending her two weeks of spring break with her parents in Italy, she wanted to spend it with me before I went on tour. So now I was on my way to the airport to pick her up.

The honk of a car horn, knocks me out of my daze down memory lane and brings me back to reality. Traffic was finally moving again. I release my foot from the brake, and I drive until I reach the airport.

* * *

Fifteen minutes later I pull into the airport, I grab a parking ticket out the machine and I find a parking spot with no problem. I run into the airport, making my way over to a set of monitors displaying flight information. I pull my phone out of my pocket and I scroll down to Nyla's flight info that she text me the other day. Finding the information I needed, I go in search for her gate. After going through obstacles of escalators, people either running into me, or not moving fast enough to a point I had to go around, I make my way to her gate and find people standing around looking at the closed door behind the airline attendant's counter.

I walk up to the counter to get flight information from the cute, but very rude attendant that I guess was pissed because she was tired of everyone asking her the same damn questions, only to be told that Nyla's flight had been delayed an hour and that it would be landing shortly.

I thanked the attendant, and she stands there looking me up and down appreciating what she saw. After a couple of seconds of her checking me out, she reaches for a pen, and scribbles something on a sheet of paper. She slid it across the counter, with a sexy look on her face. I take the slip of paper off the counter. I look down and see her name and number. Shaking my head. I look up at her and slip it into my jean's pocket, then I turn around and walk over to an empty chair, taking a seat. Five minutes later, the attendant announces the landing of Nyla's plane.

I remain seated until the door behind the counter opens, and the passengers begin making their exit. I watch as friends and families reunite with each other, while still waiting on Nyla to appear.

I continue to watch as passengers make their exit until my eyes connect with a female with shoulder length straight hair, light brown eyes, and the prettiest brown skin. *Nyla.* She smiles and starts waving in my direction, while trying to walk around other passengers to get to me. I stand there counting down the steps until she would be in my arms.

While waiting, my eyes start to reacquaint themselves with her features. She was my same Nyla. Just older, mature and of course she was beautiful. I stand there watching as she makes her way to me. Finally walking around a couple embraced in a kiss. She stops a couple of feet away from me and drops her carry-on bag on the floor. Running fast enough to not knock anyone over, she jumps into my arms and tightly wraps her arms around my neck. I return the hug by wrapping my arms around her waist, lifting her feet off the floor and pulling her to my body, with her fit curves molding against my body. It felt so good having her in my arms after all these years.

"Caleb it's so good to see you. I've missed you so much!" She says.

"I've missed you too girl. So much." I respond back with my face buried in the crook of her neck.

We stand in the same spot holding each other for what seemed like forever. Placing her feet back on the floor. We pull away from each other. I place my hands on the sides of her face and I gently rub my thumbs across her cheeks, looking down into her eyes.

"I can't believe you're here." I say loud enough for her to hear me.

"I know. Especially after all these years."

My hands fall from her face, I grab her carry-on, and I wrap my arm around her shoulder, walking her in the direction to baggage claim.

"How was your flight?" I ask her then I place a kiss to the top of her head.

"I don't know." She says with a laugh. "I slept the entire time while listening to your music; which is really great by the way."

"I know." I say in a cocky tone.

"You're a mess." She laughs. "But seriously Caleb. There wasn't a song I did not like. You are very talented. Then you have Mason...I don't know. When he sings, you

25

hear so much emotion in his voice."

"Well I'm glad you enjoyed it."

I squeeze her neck and we continue to baggage claim.

After collecting all of her bags, we load them into my Camaro and we head back to my place.

"The band is stopping by to go over some music and lyrics. If you're not up for it, let me know and we'll go somewhere else. I'm sure you're tired." I glance in her direction.

"No I'm fine, but thanks for considering my feelings."

"Of course."

"I do have a question though, and I can't believe I never asked you this until now."

"What's that?"

"How did Wildfire come about? How did you guys meet?"

"Well I met Jax my first year of college. At the time he and I were taking a math class together, and I remember sitting in that lecture listening to the professor, trying to figure out what the hell she was talking about, when I kept hearing this light tapping noise. I was already frustrated because I couldn't understand a damn thing the professor was teaching. I turned my attention to Jax getting ready to go slap the fuck off, when I noticed him scribbling down music notes. He would tap. Scribble. Tap. Scribble. After class I stopped him in the hall and introduced myself. You know how I've always wanted to be in a band, so I asked him if he ever thought about it, and that's when he told me that he was already a part of one, but some shit went down with their lead singer that put him in jail for ten years. He introduced me to brothers, Evan and Jeremy. I sang some music I was working on, and they liked me and asked me to join them. We changed the name of the band to Wildfire, and was lucky enough to pick up a few gigs at The Grind, until Sierra, the owner, wanted us to play full time. Six months into being a new band, Mason stopped by and paid us a visit out of the blue during one of our practices at the club. That fucker came in there cocky as hell. I don't know how he found out that we were practicing that night, but I'm glad he did. What blew my mind that night was that Sierra was there working on some things for the club when she heard Mason sing. She said his voice had her creaming in her panties, and she's into women. But yeah. That's how we met.

"Now you guys are about to go on tour. Amazing."

She responds.

"I know right." I say not believing how far we've come as a band.

We continue the ride to my place catching up and reminiscing about old times. I pull up into my driveway and see several cars parked on my lawn.

"I guess everyone got here early." Nyla says getting out the car.

"I guess so." I respond getting out and closing the door behind me. "I'll walk you in and I'll come back and get your bags in a minute."

"Okay."

I grab her hand and we walk up the sidewalk to my childhood home. Knowing the door would be unlocked, I turn the knob and we walk in. I release her hand and she walks into the living room.

three
Nyla

As soon as I step inside, I immediately feel at home.

"I'm going to grab your bags real quick." Caleb says from behind me.

I nod my head yes as confirmation, and I look around the open space that I considered my second home for so many years, and I'm amazed to see the place looked the same, but had a bachelor feel to it. I walk around the room, reacquainting myself with the space, stopping in front of the built in bookshelf that stored all the family pictures that were taken throughout the years. I was surprised to see that there were several pictures of me and Caleb still displayed on the shelf. My favorite one being of us at the state fair. I think we were nine at the time. We stood there with our faces decorated with face paint, giving Caleb's mom our biggest smile, while embracing each other in a hug. It's funny how at that time, kids our age thought boys or girls had cooties, but Caleb and I didn't care. We were inseparable.

Unable to stop smiling from all the memories, I glance at the next picture of a young Caleb holding a guitar bigger than him. Man did he love music. He was never the type to be interested in video games or playing sports. After school when I would go home with him, we finished our homework, had a snack, then we would find ourselves in the basement where Caleb's dad kept his music studio, making what we called music. Caleb would be messing around on his dad's bass guitar, and I would stand on a chair until I was eye level with the microphone, singing my heart out.

The sound of the door closing behind me, quickly jars me out my thoughts.

I turn my head to find Caleb standing there with his hands full with my bags. He places them on the floor and walks over to where I'm standing.

"Please tell me that you're not looking at my naked baby pictures." He says, coming up behind me.

"Actually no." I laugh. "Oh I almost forgot about this picture!" I say while pointing to a picture of Caleb grinning ear to ear, when he received his first guitar on his thirteenth birthday. "I remember you got so mad at me, because I smeared cake all over you face."

"I didn't care about the cake being on my face, I was more concerned about you getting it on my guitar."

"You and your instruments. Do you still have that

guitar?" I ask turning around to face him, not realizing how close he was standing next to me.

He tears his gaze away from the picture and looks down at me. My heart begins to pound that familiar beat caused by the way Caleb looks at me with those green eyes. I guess I shouldn't be surprised that after all this time a part, I still had a little crush on my best friend.

My gaze travels down to his perfect straight nose, all the way down to a set of perfect lips. On the corner of his bottom lip, was a lip ring that complimented his new rock look. The last time I saw Caleb, he didn't have any piercings or tattoos. Now his body was decorated in them. Over the years he would text me pictures of his newest ink or piercing. When he and some of the other band members decided to get nipple rings, he actually sent video footage of it.

"Nyla."

"Huh? I'm sorry, what did you say?"

"Are you ready to head down to the basement and meet the rest of the band?" He asks staring at me with a smirk on his face.

"Um sure. If you want, go ahead. I'm going to head to

my room and shower real quick."

"Okay, well let me help you get your bags to your room."

"Well aren't you the bestest friend ever!" I tease.

He rolls his eyes and turns around and walks over to my bags, with me right behind him.

We gather all my bags, then I follow Caleb down the hall that housed three other bedrooms. His house had a total of five bedrooms in total, that he shared with two other band members. We continue down the long hallway with Caleb several feet ahead of me when I hear someone moaning out in pleasure. I continue walking then stop when I hear it coming from the bedroom on my left. I turn my attention to the door and see it's halfway open, but open enough where I could look inside without pushing it open further to get a better view. Inside I find a guy with a red mohawk resting back on his elbows on his bed, while receiving a blow job from some girl with brunette hair.

"Watch the teeth Jess." He moans out in pleasure. "Yeah just like that baby. Fuck!" He shouts.

I stand there glued to my spot watching. *Did Caleb not hear them?* Before I could think more about what was unfolding in front of me. The guy looks up and his eyes lock with mine. He smirks at me and winks in my direction. Quickly tearing my gaze away from his I turn my attention away from the bedroom and make my way to mine, that was located right across from Caleb's.

I walk through the door and see Caleb placing my bags on the floor, and I do the same, trying to pretend that I didn't just catch one of his roommates getting head, down the hall.

"As you can see mom has redecorated since the last time you were here. There's fresh towels in your bathroom, so make yourself at home. Do you need anything before I go?"

No I'm okay. I think I can manage. I did spend most of my time here growing up, but if I need you I know where to find you."

"Okay I'll be in the basement. See you downstairs in a few."

"Ok."

He turns around and walks out the room closing the door behind him.

I look around the room that use to be Caleb's parent's before they decided to move and leave the house to him. The room had been removed of its white furniture and was replaced with dark cherry wood furnishings decorated with hints of violet accents that matched the violet comforter set.

Picking up my small luggage, I place it on the bed. I unzip it and pull out a pair of black yoga pants and my East NYU shirt, that I had cut off around the neck that exposed my shoulders every time I wore it. I grab my makeup bag, body wash, and body cream and I walk into the bathroom and I remove all my make up before hopping into the shower to wash both my hair and body.

I cut the shower off and wrap my body with a towel before heading back into my room to grab an old shirt that I use to dry my now curly hair, to prevent it from frizzing up. When I'm finished I wrap the shirt around my head and I walk back into the bathroom to dry off and lotion my body.

Once I'm done I apply a little face moisturizer, lip balm, and a dab of olive oil to my hair, then I throw on my clothes and I make my way out my room and towards the basement.

I hear the sound of laughter and voices mingling together when I finally reach the open door of the basement. Taking one step at a time, I make my way down the stairs to the basement.

As soon as my feet touch the basement floor, all conversation and laughter stops, and all attention is on me.

"Damn Caleb, is this your best friend you were tellin' us about?" The guy with long dreads and skin the color mocha asks out loud. The girl that was currently taking up time in his lap, smacked him in the back of his head, before getting off his lap, and walks over and sits down on the only vacant seat left.

I look around the room at every face staring back at me until my gaze lands on Caleb. Smiling at me, he motions me over.

"You guys this is Nyla." He says when I approach, before he pulls me onto his lap.

I look around at the shocked faces looking at me.

"Hey." I respond.

No response.

"I'm sorry, but am I missing something?" I turn around to ask Caleb.

Pulling me closer, he leans in and whispers in my ear.

"No I think it's been awhile since they've seen anyone as beautiful as you around." He says, sending chills throughout my body.

"Um excuse me, but Caleb are you going to introduce us?" The one with the dreads speaks up again.

Caleb clears his throat. "Yeah. Nyla the one who's been running his mouth since you came down here is Jax, the lead drummer of our band."

"Sup girl." Jax responds.

"The one with the fire red mohawk is Evan. He's the roommate I've been telling you about, and he's our rhythmic guitarist."

We've sort of already met. I think to myself. But I sit there and pretend I never witnessed what I saw earlier.

"Nice to meet you Nyla." He smiles and laughs as if he were reading my mind.

"You have Jeremy here. Supposedly he's the musical genius of our group that can play any instrument he can get his hands on."

I look at Jeremy and notice his gorgeous blue eyes, killer dimples, and long straight black hair. He winks, then waves at me.

"And I would introduce you to Mason but he had to rush and pick his sister Brooke up who had car trouble, so he should be here in a few."

"Okay. Well it's nice to finally meet all of you." I respond with a smile.

"Ha. So what makes her so fuckin' special Caleb that you can't introduce us?" The girl I saw earlier with Evan asks from her position on his lap.

I look at her and catch her sizing me up with a look of disgust on her too much, make up covered face. Her brunette hair was pulled up into a high pony tail, and she was lounging around in a large t shirt and I wasn't sure if she was wearing anything underneath it.

I change my position on Caleb's lap and I face her, getting ready to give her a piece of my mind, when I hear someone coming down the stairs. I look towards the stairs and see a guy descending them. When he makes it to the bottom he's greeted by everyone around him, except me.

37

"About fuckin' time man!" Evan speaks out. He stands and playfully ruffles the guy's already ruffled dark hair, then pulls him into a brief head lock.

"That's Mason." Caleb says behind me.

After Evan releases Mason from the headlock. Mason comes to a full standing position and runs his hands through his hair and turns his attention to Jeremy and Jax. Giving them both a special hand shake they only knew.

"Nyla." I hear Caleb again.

"Huh?" I respond without turning around, because my eyes were still glued on Mason. As if he could feel my eyes on him, he turns his head while still listening to whatever Jeremy was saying to him and his eyes lock with mine.

"I need you to get up for a sec." Caleb continues.

Tearing my eyes away from a pair of gray ones. I stand and remove myself off Caleb's lap. Caleb walks over to Mason and shares the same handshake. I sit down on the couch looking at them. They exchange several words with each other, before turning their attention to me.

"Nyla this is Mason our lead vocalist, and Mason this is

my best friend I've been telling you about.

He doesn't say anything but stares, and gives me a half smile, showing off his dimples.

"Hey." I respond.

"Well I'm still waiting on my introduction!" Jess yells.

"I got this Nyla." Jax speaks up. "Why are you here Jess?" Jax continues.

"You know why I'm here." She responds licking her lips while looking in Mason's direction.

"How many times has Mason turned your ass down? Fuck I wouldn't want you after all the dicks you've had in yo mouth."

"Don't knock it until you try me." She responds.

"No thank you." Jax responds laughing.

"I still want you babe." Evan responds pulling her close to him, just to be pushed away by her. She stands abruptly and the girl that took the last seat in the room stands with her. "I'm out. Sasha are you ready?" She asks the girl.

"Yeah." Sasha responds with her arms folded across her chest.

"Good because we have work to do." Jax says.

"Fuck you Jax." Jess says before stomping up the stairs, with her friend right behind her.

Caleb resumes his spot on the couch and I scoot away to give him some space. Mason grabs the vacant chair and sits it on the other side of Caleb.

"So now that we got that out the way. Caleb how about you explain to us why you never told us that Nyla was so damn fine!"

"Whatever man." Caleb laughs beside me.

"I would like to know the answer to that question myself." Jeremy says with a huge grin on his face.

"You guys have been friends this long, and you've never tried hittin' that?" Evan asks next.

"Yo!" Caleb shouts. He laughs then continues. "We've got work to do."

"Man this conversation isn't over." Evan responds.

I start to stand, but Caleb pulls me back down onto the couch.

"Where are you going?" He asks me.

"I'm going upstairs so you can finish up."

"No, stay." He responds. "We're just going over some lyrics. You don't have to move."

"Okay."

I turn around and see Jax, Evan, Mason and Jeremy looking at the both of us.

Caleb was either totally unaware of their stares or he didn't care continues. "Last night Mason and I were looking over the pieces and we were thinking. Instead of sharing the music we wrote for the tour, we could do our own covers and renditions of *Lollipop* sung by *Framing Hanley* and *The Crow & The Butterfly* by *Shinedown*. Evan I want you to take lead guitar on *Lollipop* and I'll finish it up with *The Crow & The Butterfly*.

"Cool with me." Evan responds.

"Jax and Jeremy. Any suggestions or are we cool?"

Caleb ask.

"Let's do the damn thang!" Jax responds.

"I'm with Jax." Jeremy replies.

"Alright. Let's do this." Caleb says.

I release a yawn and change my position on the couch, giving me a good view of Mason. My eyes linger on his full lips that housed two corner lip rings on his bottom lip, moving down to the decorative ink tatted on his neck. His tatted elbows were resting against his long legs and he was currently looking over the lyrics of the songs they were performing for tomorrow night. From time to time he would flip the pages back and forth while trying to memorize the lyrics, causing the lean muscles in his arms to tense up. He was currently bobbing his head up and down, listening to the beats Jax was creating, while tapping his own pen against the papers in his hands. He senses my eyes on him again, because he stops, turns his head and looks at me. Locking his eyes with mine. For a brief moment I saw something deliciously dangerous in his eyes. After a moment of staring at each other, he breaks eye contact with me and continues studying the music.

I lay my head against the cushion and I close my eyes listening to Mason and Jax go over the beats. I inhale deeply catching Caleb's scent. A mixture of cedar wood, lavender, or maybe it was vanilla. Whatever it was, it immediately relaxes me even more. It didn't help that my body was still operating on New York's time zone.

A light rhythmic beat, causes me to open my eyes to see Jax with a pair of drum sticks hitting against a rubber practice drum pad, beating out the required beats for the song.

The sound of Mason's voice going over the lyrics with Caleb, has me closing my eyes again, and eventually drifting off to sleep.

four
Mason

A satisfied moan slips from my lips when I feel something rub along the front of my pants and against my dick, that has it stirring immediately in my pants. Groaning in pleasure, I slowly open my eyes and see Nyla laying beside me, stretching her arms above her head. She arches her back, causing her ass to rub against my erection even more. *I know she had to feel it.* I gently place my hand on her hip to still her movement.

She tenses up and turns around slowly, causing another moan to slip from my lips.

"Good morning." I say through gritted teeth, trying to hide the desire in my voice.

"What time is it?" She sits up quickly to a sitting position. "How did we end up like this? I can't believe we fell asleep down here."

Good question. I thought to myself. I remembered swapping seats with Caleb so he and Jax could go over the beats of the music. I remember closing my eyes briefly. Listening to all the sounds around me, and I guess that's

44

when I fell asleep. Now how I ended up laying behind Nyla was a mystery to me.

"Me either." I respond closing my eyes briefly.

I reach into my back pocket, pulling my phone out to check the time, just to see several missed text messages from my sister.

"It's twelve thirty."

"In the afternoon? We slept that long?" She asks me.

"I guess we did." I respond.

I adjust myself in my pants and I come to a sitting position beside her.

"I've got to be going." I say slowly coming to my feet. "I've got to get my sister to her class. Then I have to work on her car. She's probably wondering where I am."

"Class?" Nyla asks.

"Yeah. You know college." I say trying not to sound sarcastic.

"I'm sorry." She responds. "I just assumed everyone

was on spring break. I keep forgetting I live on the other side of the United States. I didn't mean to be so nosey." She says coming to her feet.

"Forget about it." I say shaking my head to myself, while walking towards the stairs. "Oh and sorry about this morning. I haven't been getting enough sleep lately. I crashed and somehow ended up behind you on the couch."

"Forget about it." She responds in a teasing tone.

Step by step I begin making my way up the stairs.

"Hey Mason." Nyla calls behind me.

"Yeah?" I respond turning around to give her my full attention.

"I'm going to the store to get some things for a late breakfast. Did you want to stick around? If you want, you can take some to your sister."

I stand there looking at a beautiful girl that I knew little about, and she knew nothing about me and how fucked up I thought my life was right now, offer to cook me and my sister breakfast.

"Thanks Nyla, but I really need to be going."

"Okay." She responds giving me a smile.

I tear my attention away and continue up the stairs and out the front door until I'm safe behind the wheel of my late model black Mustang.

* * *

I turn off the paved road and onto a dirt road leading down a long winding one surrounded by nothing but trees, until I pull up into my Grandma's yard.

My grandma's car was nowhere in sight. I cut my engine off and hop out of my car. Walking up several stairs to the three-bedroom brick house that my grandma owned, I open the screen door and unlock the front door.

I walk in and can smell the scent of stale cigarettes lingering in the air. Even after my grandma was diagnosed with lung cancer a year ago, she still continued to smoke.

"Mason, I've lived a long healthy life. I'm already dying so why should I stop?"

Were her words exactly.

I close the door and lock it behind me.

"Brooke!" I yell my sister's name out.

"I'm getting dressed!" She yells from the other side of the house.

I walk into the kitchen and I see pots and pans with yesterday's food still inside and dirty dishes in the sink soaking in soapy water.

Walking over to the refrigerator I see a note posted from my grandma intended for Brooke stating that she went to the grocery store and pharmacy, and that she'll return shortly. Grabbing the note off the fridge, I crumble it up and toss it in the trash before making my way to my old bedroom.

"Did you see the note from ma?" I ask Brooke, while standing outside her bedroom door. I didn't know much about my mom except that she was doing time for attempted murder and possession of drugs and she had several years left before she got out. So I always referred to my grandma as ma for short, because not only was she my grandma, but she was like a mom to me.

"Yeah I got it." Brooke responds on the other side.

"Okay. I'm going to get in the shower. Be ready in twenty. I don't want you to be late for school."

"Alright already." She responds.

I walk in my room and go straight for the closet. I grab some clothes that I still haven't had time to move to my new residence. Then I grab a pair of boxers out my dresser and I make my way back down the hall to the bathroom.

I strip out of my clothes dreading the cold shower I was going to have to take to relieve this ache in my dick.

Fuck a cold shower.

I pull back the shower curtain and I turn on the faucet and adjust it to a comfortable temp. I get in and allow the warm water to stream down my body. Resting one hand against the shower wall, I close my eyes and grab my dick with the other. It was so hard that it hurt.

I close my eyes and I think about the girl with the beautiful brown skin, lips, fit curves, and smile. Just meeting her on yesterday, I could see Nyla was beautiful both inside and out. I can see why Caleb remained friends with her after all these years apart.

Trying to relieve the ache that I was feeling hanging between my legs, I begin to slowly stroke myself. I couldn't believe the affect Nyla was having on me. When I first laid eyes on her, I knew I was in trouble. She was different from the women I usually deal with. *What was it?* Maybe it was the way she closed her eyes and swayed back and forth when I would sing the lyrics to the songs we were working on. Like she could feel every emotion I was feeling through the lyrics. That had to be it, because the females that I've come in contact with lately wanted one thing from me. *Me.* Anyway they could have me. I'm not complaining about the amount of pussy I get. Hell no. But it would be nice to have someone that really appreciated what I was all about for a change. But then again. I didn't know much about Nyla except from the conversations I've had with Caleb about her, to our first brief meeting.

"Fuck." I say, leaning my head against the tile.

Clenching my stomach muscles, I grip myself a little harder and begin massaging a good rhythm up and down my dick. I was so close. I could feel it.

It was probably best I stayed away. I had enough going on in my life. If I let her in, it would only bring her down with me, and I couldn't do that to her.

But she could *be a good distraction...*

Maybe I could call the cute little blonde I fucked a couple a nights ago, that I met at the club. What was her name again? Was it Cassie? It didn't matter. Right now I needed something other than my hand.

I close my eyes and imagine Cassie on her knees in front of me, doing all the sinful things she knew she could do with her mouth. Just the thought of how she swirls her tongue and suck me into her mouth, wasn't working because my mind kept drifting back to Nyla. All of a sudden Cassie's face was replaced by Nyla's. Instead of Cassie's lips wrapped around me, they were Nyla's.

Moaning, I pick the speed up, and begin stroking myself harder, until I'm able to finally find my release. Coming so hard, I almost slip in the shower. My mouth parts open, and Nyla's name slip through my lips.

Finishing up I lay my head against the tile, breathing hard. I close my eyes until I'm able to slow my heart rate down, and even out my breathing. I open my eyes and reach for my body wash. I pour some onto my wash cloth and begin lathering up my body.

After rinsing off I grab my shampoo and quickly wash my hair. I lower my head under the water and rinse it out before shutting the shower off. I slide the shower curtain open and I grab my towel off the hook. I dry off and wrap the towel around my waist.

Standing in front of the sink, I wipe my hand across the fogged up mirror until I'm able to see my reflection. I stand there for several minutes looking at myself trying to figure out what the fuck I was going to do about my sudden attraction to my band mate's best friend, Nyla.

five
caleb

I stop in the doorway of the kitchen watching Nyla go through the refrigerator. The shirt she was wearing was currently exposing her right shoulder. She was reaching in the refrigerator, rummaging through whatever she was looking for.

She closes the refrigerator and turns around, and our eyes meet.

"Why are you looking at me like that?" She asks me.

"Yeah man why are you looking at her like that?"

I turn around and I see Evan smiling at me. He walks around me and takes a seat on one of the bar stools at the island counter.

"Good morning Nyla." He says.

"Good morning Evan. Are you hungry?"

"Starving." He responds.

Ignoring him and her question, I walk around the kitchen island, until I'm standing in front of her.

"What are you cooking? It smells good."

"Well. While you still sleeping, I borrowed your car and went to the store to get what I needed to make your favorite. Strawberry pancakes. I hope they come out right." She smiles up at me.

Grabbing her hand, I pull her closer to my body and into a hug. "You didn't have to do that. You're the best." I say before kissing the top of her head.

"Are you hungry?" She asks me, then pulls away and walks over to the stove.

I walk around the island and I take a seat on the stool beside Evan.

"Actually I am."

"Okay, everything will be ready soon." She says.

She turns around and begins pouring pancake batter in the skillet. She reaches for the spatula and stands there for a moment, before flipping the pancake over.

"Don't you have somewhere to be?" I ask turning my attention to Evan.

"Chill dude. I just want some pancakes and I'll be out your way. Nyla is it alright if I have some of your pancakes?" He asks, totally insinuating something else.

"Of course Evan. There's plenty. Matter of fact there will be enough to refrigerate for later."

"Well I can't wait to taste them." Evan says enunciating the word taste a little too much.

"If you don't shut the fuck up." I say low enough for Evan to hear.

"Okay man. I'm just playing." He laughs. "So Nyla do you have a boyfriend?"

Shaking my head, I turn my attention to Nyla, because I was on the verge of knocking his ass off the stool.

Turning around, she places a plate full of pancakes in front of me and Evan.

"No I'm single."

"Really? Why is that?"

"I date, but I just haven't found someone special enough to share my time with."

"Well maybe I'm special enough." He responds.

"Evan." I say his name in warning.

"Okay fine." He says with a mouth full of pancakes. "The food is delicious by the way Nyla." He says picking his plate up. "I'll be in the basement if you guys need me."

He leaves and Nyla takes his seat beside me with a plate of her own pancakes.

"How are they?"

"Damn girl these are really good." I respond with a mouth full.

"I'm glad you like them."

"You did your thang." I agreed.

We sit there eating in silence until both of our plates are empty.

"That was so good. I am so stuffed. You mind helping me load the dishwasher?" She asks me.

"Actually I have to get going. I've got to meet with Sierra. We have a couple of things to go over about tonight."

She gathers our plates and takes them to the sink to rinse them off.

"Are we riding to the club together tonight?" She asks me.

"I've got to leave here a little early before everyone starts showing up. So I'll leave my keys here with you."

"Okay, cool. I can't wait to hear you guys play tonight. Are you excited?"

"I'm not trying to sound cocky but this is nothing new to me."

"Maybe that will change once you start performing in front of larger crowds."

"Maybe."

"You'll see."

"I'll see you later Nyla. Thanks for breakfast. It was really good."

I walk around the counter and I kiss her on the forehead. Then I grab my keys and head out the door passing Mason on the way out.

six
Nyla

Singing the lyrics to one of Wildfire's songs I had memorized from my plane ride yesterday, I place the last dish into the dishwasher. Reaching under the sink I grab the detergent and I pour it into the dispenser and I close the door and press start. I grab the plate of uneaten pancakes and I turn around and almost drop them when I see Mason standing there looking at me with an amused look on his gorgeous face.

I place the plate down on the counter and I look up at Mason.

"How long have you been standing there?"

"Long enough to hear that awesome finale to our song. You have a nice voice by the way." He says with a smile on his face.

"Whatever. I thought I was the only one here." I say while looking into his unusual light gray eyes.

"Nope. It looks like it's just you and me." He says

staring at my lips. Are these for me?" He asks now looking down at the plate of pancakes.

"Yeah if you want them. I was getting ready to put them in the refrigerator."

"I'm starving."

"Here let me heat them up for you."

I grab the plate and I put it into the microwave.

"I hope you're not allergic to strawberries."

"I'm not allergic to anything."

"Good. Then I hope you enjoy the pancakes."

"I'm sure I will."

I turn around waiting on the microwave to stop. I could still feel his eyes on me. When the microwave chimes I put the warm plate of pancakes along with the syrup, and a fork in front of Mason.

He picks up the fork and dives in without putting syrup on them. He closes his eyes and moans. The sound alone sends a chill down my spine. He opens his eyes and continues chewing.

"These are really good Nyla. I'm not going to lie. Sharing a house full of men. You find days when you don't get a good home cooked meal. Where did you learn how to make these?"

"Caleb's mom. Those are his favorite." I say pointing at his plate.

"Well they're now mine." He says digging his fork in for more. "No syrup needed." He says before stuffing his mouth again.

"I'm glad you like them." I respond with my eyes trained on his mouth. "So what are your plans for today?"

"As soon as I'm done eating. I'm heading back to my shop to finish working on my sister's car."

"Are you a mechanic?"

"Something like that. I work on cars from time to time to bring in some extra cash, when we're not performing at the club. My grandma doesn't work right now, but she gets a monthly disability check from the government that isn't enough to take care of half our bills, plus I had to find a way to pay for tuition fees that my sister's grants and student loans wouldn't cover. So when someone needs work done on their car, motorcycle, or whatever. They usually bring it to me."

"Really? So where's your shop located?"

"It sits on my grandma's property behind her house. Maybe I'll show it to you some time."

"I would like that." I stand there looking at him longer then I should. "Well I have some more unpacking to do. Is there anything else I can get for you? Milk, water, or coffee?"

"No. But thank you."

"You're welcome."

I push away from the counter and I make my way to my room.

* * *

I pull Caleb's Camaro into the parking spot and turn the engine off. I was already running late, because I couldn't find the club. After pulling over on the side of the road, I pulled out my phone and looked at the directions that Caleb sent to me earlier to find that I punched the address into the

GPS wrong. With a deep sigh I get out of the car, and I close the door behind me.

Pulling at the hem of my blue bandage dress down a little, I quickly walk across the parking lot, careful not to twist my ankle in these high ass heels. I really wanted to look good tonight for Wildfire's last performance. So I ended up going to the mall and bought a new dress and heels that were now starting to hurt my feet.

Caleb told me to let the bouncer on duty know who I was when I got here, and they would let me in with no problem. Walking to the front of the club, I see a bouncer dressed in all black holding a clip board. There was a group of people standing in front of him, waiting for a chance to get inside the club.

"Hey excuse me."

The bouncer looks up from his clip board and looks at me.

"You must be Nyla." He says. "Caleb told me that you were on your way. He told me to tell you to go straight to the bar and ask for Sierra, and she'll take care of you."

"Thank you."

"No problem sweetheart."

He opens the door for me, and I walk in.

The moment I step in the club, the sounds of an electric guitar, drums, and people screaming fill the room. My attention is immediately drawn to a strong sexy raspy voice echoing throughout the club. My eyes begin to search the room, looking for the owner of the voice, when they finally land on Mason. He's standing behind the microphone with his eyes closed, grasping it while letting the lyrics flow through his lips. Every emotion he was feeling came flowing.

Women were screaming his name, demanding his attention, while the men stood in awe wishing they could be him. I stood still not wanting to move, afraid that I would miss the message he was trying to get across in the lyrics. I'd never been a fan of rock music, but then again I really didn't have a favorite genre either. If it was good to me I listened to it, and Wildfire was good.

He stops singing and pulls away from the mic. He picks up an acoustic guitar sitting on its stand nearby and starts playing it with so much grace. I couldn't take my eyes off of him. Seeing him perform gave me an amazing feeling. I've always relied on video clips and audio snippets Caleb sent to me by text of Mason's musical talent, and now I'm able to experience it live.

Everything about Mason oozed sex appeal from his tousled black hair, all the way down to his exposed neck, arms and legs, that showed off his different tats, to the way he worked the crowd. Flirting with every male or female he came in contact with. He didn't discriminate.

He was now making his way back to the mic, and when he does, he closes his eyes briefly again and begins rocking back and forth, allowing the music to take over him. Before singing the next verse of the song, he opens his eyes and they lock with mine. From that single moment alone, I became his number one fan.

I stand there getting lost in his gray eyes. His eyes never once turned away from mine, while he continued to sing verse after verse. My eyes linger down to his lips and I watch the lyrics to their rendition of **The Crow & The Butterfly** slip through his lips as if the song was made for him. He took control of the song and made it his own. My eyes linger back up his to find they were still on me. *Was he singing to me?* The club was packed, so it could be anyone around me that he was looking at. I chance a glance at my surroundings and see everyone's attention on the stage. *Yeah it could be anyone.* I think to myself. I turn my attention back to the stage and my eyes meet once again with Mason's. This time he has a sexy smirk on his face. He winks in my direction and before directing his attention to the other screaming fans around him. Not wanting to leave my spot, I eventually tear my gaze away from him, and I make my way to the bar, taking a seat on the bar stool.

"What can I get for you beautiful?"

My attention falls on a pair of blue eyes belonging to a female that looked to be in her early thirties with shoulder length red hair.

"I'm looking for Sierra." I shout over the music.

"You're talking to her." She says leaning on the counter.

"I'm Nyla. Caleb's friend. I was told to ask for you."

Sierra stands there looking at me for a moment, sizing me up. She hops on the bar and swings her legs around and hops down and stands beside me.

"Let's go Doll Face."

Doll Face?

I follow behind Sierra, looking around her at the stage to find Mason working the crowd once again, now shirtless showing off his lean muscles and tatted skin. As we get closer, my eyes slowly travel down the length of his sweaty body, noticing the way his jeans clung to his narrow hips, showing off his V cut and well defined abs.

"Is this your first time hearing Wildfire perform live?" Sierra yells.

"Yes." I shout back unable to tear my eyes away from Mason.

We continue to walk to the front stopping at a booth near the stage.

Sierra turns around and looks at me.

"Caleb wants you to sit right here. Can I get you something to drink?"

"Can I get a Cola?"

"Coming right up Doll Face."

She turns around and walks back to the bar.

My attention goes back to the stage, and I catch Mason staring at me. He hops off the stage and begins making his way through the crowd. Females were reaching out touching him and pulling on him, only to be pulled back by the bouncers standing close by. He's making his way in my direction when a female with long blonde hair steps out in front of him. She pulls his face to hers, pulling his attention away from me and kisses him. Eventually she pulls away and rubs her thumb against his lips to remove any lipstick she left behind. They stand there for a minute looking at each other until Mason looks up and his eyes lock with mine. The blonde turns around and looks at me. She turns back around and turns his face back to hers. She places another kiss to his lips, then turns around and begins grinding her ass against him. The club gets loud from the show being put on in front of them. Mason places his hands on her hips and starts matching her movements. She leans forward causing her skirt to ride up on her thighs, giving him better access to whatever was under her skirt. Was she wearing underwear? I'm sure he knew.

Sierra returns with my drink and places it on the table. "Here you go Doll Face. Can I get you anything else?"

I tear my gaze away from Mason and up to Sierra.

"No. Thanks Sierra. Can you point me in the direction to the bathroom?"

"Sure they're right over there in the far corner." She says pointing behind me.

"Thanks."

I turn around, but before I can move any further a hand grabs a hold of mine. I turn around and I see Caleb standing there with a smile on his face.

The music starts to pick up and I look up and see Evan taking over the stage with Jax beating hard on his drums, while Jeremy played the hell out of his electric guitar. Evan stands in the middle of the stage and removes his shirt. Throwing it into the crowd, then he starts singing **Lollipop**.

Caleb tugs on my hand, bringing my attention back to him. He turns around and walks us closer to the stage. He pulls me closer to his body then he places my arms around his neck, and wraps his arms around my waist.

"You look really beautiful tonight." He says in my ear.

"Thank you. This is a big night for you guys, and I wanted to look nice."

"Well you look better than nice. You know you're wearing my favorite color right?" He says running his hand along my bare back, from where the dress dipped low in the back, exposing practically my whole back. "I wanted to apologize to you for this morning. I hope I didn't come off as being rude. I just had a lot to do today before tonight."

"You don't have to explain. I accept your apology." I respond looking at his shirtless body that was covered in sweat.

"Are you having fun?" He asks me pulling my attention away from his body.

"I am, but I wish I could have gotten here earlier, but I got lost. Don't ask me how I did, but I got here as quick as I could."

"I'm just glad you made it."

"Me too." I say looking up into his eyes.

"I've got to get back on stage, I just wanted to come down to apologize and say hello."

"Okay." I respond.

He starts to walk back to the stage but turns around.

"Hey. Tomorrow just you and me. We'll do whatever you want. I haven't been much of a friend since you got here. So I think we should put some time aside and catch up."

"I agree." I respond with a sincere smile. I turn my head and see Mason staring at us with a look of curiosity on his face.

"Hey." Caleb says my name, getting my attention. "Be careful."

"What are you talking about?"

"I've been watching and I've noticed that Mason has taken interest in you. He's my boy, but I know how he works okay."

"Caleb what makes you think I'm interested in him?"

Leaning forward he continues. "I'm not blind Nyla. You're just like all the many girls that go crazy over him. I'm not trying to tell you who you should see and who you shouldn't, but again I've known him for a while. You mean the world to me and I would hate to see you get hurt. Even if you want to deny that you aren't interested. Just be careful. That's all I'm going to say." He says into my ear. "Meet me at the bar in a few minutes." He tilts my head back and leans down and kisses me on my cheek. He pulls away and runs then jumps back on stage.

Leaving me standing there speechless.

To my surprise, he grabs the microphone from Evan and finishes off the song.

I turn around and I walk to the bathroom.

I walk inside and into a stall. I'm fixing my dress when I hear a group of girls walk in.

"Who was that bitch Mason was checking out?"

"Who fuckin' cares. I'm sure I won't have any problems getting him in my bed tonight. Especially how I put it on him the last time. I don't even think he's into black girls any way."

"You're probably right Cassie."

"Again, I can care less."

Having heard enough of what the bitch had to say. I step out of the stall and make my way to the sink next to her. I wash my hands and I dry them off. Quickly I finger comb through my curly strands. I open my clutch and pull out my nude lip gloss that looked good against my brown skin, and I apply some to my lips. Putting my gloss back, I make sure my mascara wasn't smudged under my eyes, and I turn my attention to the bitch that was currently glaring me down.

Her friend stood behind her not saying a word.

"Do I know you?" I ask her.

She stands there quiet like her scared friend.

"That's what I thought. So I advise you to keep anything you have to say about me out your mouth."

With those last words I walk out the bathroom.

I make my way to the bar, and as I get closer I see Wildfire sitting around the counter with a girl or two sitting in their laps, and some were surrounding them.

"There she is." Sierra exclaims when she sees me. "Doll Face come on over here."

I walk behind the counter and stand beside Sierra. She throws her arm around my shoulder and continues.

"Now I want you to listen to me." She says directing her attention to Wildfire. "I'm going to really miss you guys. Even though some of you were the reason to why I lost some of my female employees because you couldn't keep your dicks in your pants, and you ended up breaking their hearts in the end."

"Now Sierra, I'm sorry for interrupting you." Jax speaks up. "But how do you know they weren't breaking our hearts?"

"Don't give me that shit Jax, now shut the fuck up and let me finish." She says pointing in his direction. "I have eyes and I know you guys are some good looking men. Am I right ladies?" She asks the ladies sitting around the counter. "Shit if I wasn't into women, I would probably fuck you too, but that's not the point."

Everyone, including me burst out laughing.

"The point is, that I'm truly going to miss you fuckers, and I don't ever want you to feel you can't stop by and perform every once in a while when you're not on the road touring or creating big hits. Okay?" She says almost in tears.

They all mumbled their okays and yeses to Sierra.

"Now that I got that out the way, Mason how about you bring your sexy ass around here and help us welcome Doll Face to the club."

"Wait a minute. What are you talking about?" I ask no one in particular.

"Body shots, body shots, body shots!" The other

members of the band, begin to chant.

I look at Caleb, and he has a smirk on his face.

I stand there curious. Wondering what's about to happen next.

I watch as Mason stands and walks behind the counter in my direction, coming into my personal space.

"It's okay honey. It's tradition. We always let Mason welcome all the new beauties to the club. What do you have a taste for Mason." Sierra asks beside me.

"Tequila." He responds.

Mason pushes my hair to the side, exposing the left side of my neck.

"Relax Nyla." He whispers in my ear.

Sierra places a bowl of limes, a salt shaker, and a bottle of tequila on the counter.

Mason takes a piece of lime and rubs it along my neck. "This might get a little messy." He says with a laugh.

"You think?" I laugh nervously.

After rubbing the lime against my neck, he places it between my lips, then picks up the salt shaker and shakes a small amount of salt on my neck. Evan pours the tequila into a shot glass, and hands it to Mason.

"Ready?" He asks me.

I shake my head yes.

He tilts my head back, and lowers his head and slowly licks the salt off my neck. My eyes slowly close shut and a moan escapes my lips. He pulls away and grabs the shot glass off the counter and drinks the tequila in one gulp. He slams the glass down, and my eyes open.

Placing both of his hands to the sides of my face, he lowers his head again and sucks the lime from between my lips, and into his mouth. He removes the lime from his mouth and leans forward and places a kiss to the side of my neck. His lips brush against my neck, working their way up to my ear.

"Welcome to The Grind Nyla." He whispers in my ear.

I grab a hold to his shirt, clutching to it tight.

"Fuck that was hot!" I hear a female customer say

behind me.

Hell yeah it was.

"Nyla look at me."

I look up and he gently brushes my cheeks with his calloused thumbs.

Looking down at me, he lowers his head and presses his lips against my ear.

"Do you want to get out of here?" He asks me.

I glance over his shoulder before answering.

"Do you think it would be right to leave your girlfriend here?"

He turns around and sees Cassie sitting on the stool he vacated, staring at the both of us, and she was pissed.

"Nyla..."

"Maybe next time Mason."

I walk around him and make my way from behind the counter, past Cassie, totally ignoring her ass. I walk around the counter and I take a seat beside Caleb.

Caleb stops talking to the pretty brunette sitting on his lap.

"You alright? Want me to order you a drink?" He asks me.

"Sure." I respond while watching Mason and Cassie in a heated discussion. I couldn't hear them, but looking at their actions I'm sure they were discussing what just happened behind the bar.

Mason leans in and whispers something in her ear. She smiles then slides her arm around his. They walk around the bar, stopping briefly to speak with Evan. Without a second glance from Mason in my direction, he leaves the club with Cassie by his side.

After an hour of sitting at the bar talking to Caleb and Jax, and watching both Jeremy and Evan throw back shots after shots of tequila, I decide to call it a night.

"Good night everyone." I say standing from the bar stool.

"Doll Face you heading out?" Sierra asks.

"Yeah I'm out." I respond. "Caleb are you riding with me?"

"Go ahead. I'm going to stick around a bit. The way Jeremy and Evan have been throwing them back. It's safe to say that I'll be there DD tonight."

"Okay. I'll see you later."

"Later." He responds back.

After I say my final goodbyes I walk out the club and hop into Caleb's Camaro. Cranking the car up, the sound of rock music comes through the speakers. I put on my seat belt, put the car in drive and pull out the parking lot, enjoying the sound of the V8 engine.

seven
Mason

When I left the club I was mad as fuck. Why did Cassie get drunk knowing damn well she wouldn't be able to drive home? I should have called a cab for her since she claimed her ride left her. Now I was on the side of the road trying to change a fuckin flat tire in the dark. The street lights on the street weren't helping, and I had no flash light. *Fuck!*

With nothing else to do, I sit on the hood of my car with nothing but my thoughts. Looking in the distance I see a set of headlights heading in my direction. I hop off my car and start yelling and waving my hands to flag the car down for help. They pass me but then the car slows down and does a U-turn in the road heading back in my direction. As the car comes into view I realize that I recognize the car. *Caleb.*

His car stops a couple of feet behind mine. The headlights dim, and the driver side door opens.

"Mason are you alright?"

"Nyla?" I whisper to myself.

She shuts her door and runs in my direction.

"What happened?" She asks me, while looking me over to see if I was hurt.

"I'm fine. It's just a flat. It's so fuckin' dark out here that I can't see so I can't change it." I respond with irritation in my voice.

"I'll help you change it."

"What?" I question.

"You heard me."

She turns around and walks back to Caleb's car and cuts the headlights on.

"Is that enough light?" She yells from the open door.

I look down and can finally see my tire.

"Yeah." I yell back.

I squat down and grab the lug wrench I had laying on the road beside my tire, and I begin loosening the screws.

Nyla kneels down beside me and watches me.

"How long have you been out here?" She asks me.

"Maybe an hour." I respond in frustration.

I continue to turn the wrench but the screw wouldn't budge.

"Shit!" I yell throwing the wrench down. "The fuckin' lug nut is on too tight."

I come to a standing position and immediately notice the silence between us.

I turn around and see Nyla standing there with a look of concern on her face.

"I'm sorry. I didn't mean to yell. I've been having a really rough week."

"I understand. I guess we'll have to leave your car here and call a tow truck in the morning." She responds giving me a small smile. "Come on I'll take us home."

She turns around and walks back to Caleb's car. I jog up behind her, and I stop her before she can get into the car.

"Let me drive."

She turns around and looks up at me.

"Do you have somewhere to be?" I ask her.

"No." She responds shaking her head.

"Come on. I have something I want to show you. I promise I won't keep you out too late."

Her eyes linger over my face for several seconds before she responds.

"Okay."

She walks around the car to the passenger side and gets in.

I jog back to my car and make sure all my doors are locked and that I have all my belongings.

I get in Caleb's car and I rev the engine up.

"I've always loved his car." I say getting a smile out of Nyla. "Are you ready?"

"Yeah I'm ready." She laughs out.

I pull out onto the road and make a sharp U-turn, heading in the opposite direction to a place I've never shared with anyone before. Until now.

eight
Nyla

I'm sitting in the passenger seat, looking out the window at our surroundings while listening to the roar of the V8 engine, as we cruise the vacant streets. After several minutes of going over bridges, and traveling down winding roads, Mason cuts on the high beams and pulls onto a dark dirt road, slowing his speed so he could maneuver around branches, holes, and the bumpy surface.

"I hope I'm not scaring you." He breaks his silence.

"No. But it would be nice if you could tell me where we're going." I say looking around the dark space.

"You're safe. I come out here all the time when I need to clear my head." He says as we continue down the dark road.

"If you make this right up here." He says pointing towards another dirt road. "Go all the way down and you'll find my grandma's house. It's the third house on the right."

"How long have you lived here? In Sacramento I mean." I ask looking in his direction.

"Practically all my life." He responds.

"I don't remember you. Did you attend school in this area?"

"No. Before my grandma adopted me and my sister. We both lived with my mom on the west side of Sacramento."

"Oh." I respond wondering what kind of life he must have lived.

The car starts to slow down a little more. I tear my gaze away from Mason and at the view in front of us. When the car comes to a stop. Mason cuts the engine, and gets out the car. I open my door, but before I could get out on my own, Mason is already there helping me out. Shutting my door, he places his hand at the small of my back and walks me to the front of the car.

"Watch your step." He says beside me.

We stop in front of the car and I can't help but to notice how beautiful and peaceful the view was.

The sky was dark, and the only light around us came from the moon shining bright, reflecting itself off the lake water in front of us.

"What do you think?" Mason asks, coming to stand beside me, leaning his weight against his car.

"Peaceful." I respond.

"That's why I love coming out here. You're the only one that I've shared my secret spot with."

"Why is that?"

"To tell you the truth. I don't know. Call me crazy, but there's something about you. I just haven't figured it out yet."

I look around the lake at the many trees surrounding it while getting lost in the calmness of the place.

"Do you come out here often?"

"Just about. I have a lot going on right now, so I'm out here almost every day. Rain or shine. It beats trying to solve my problems with booze and sex."

I look at him kind of concerned and shocked at the same time. I stare at him, trying to choose the right way to respond to his confession.

"Someone like you, I would think you would enjoy having a different girl in his bed from time to time. I mean you're a lead singer of a band. I bet you have girls fighting for your attention all the time."

He turns and looks at me with those dangerous gray eyes of his. His eyes stay locked on mine for a couple of seconds before they travel down to my mouth, and down the length of my body.

"Well when your grandma busts up into your room and finds you in bed with two girls you don't remember taking home with you. There's beer bottles everywhere and used condoms and wrappers thrown on the floor and on the bed. Your grandma is yelling and wondering why you would disrespect her house after all she's done for you. Does that sound like something you would enjoy?"

"I'm sorry Mason. I didn't mean..."

"Nyla. No worries. I was the one who fucked up. Me and my grandma are on good terms now. It happened a year ago. I was young and stupid at the time. Unlike some people, I've learned from my mistakes."

"Well that's good to know." I respond, trying to bring some type of humor into our conversation.

After a couple of seconds, we both bust out laughing.

"So what do you have going on in your life that you have to come out to this beautiful place?"

I turn my head to look at him and I catch him looking out at the water with a blank expression on his face.

My eyes wander over what I thought were perfect features. His short black hair was ruffled into a messy look. He had a perfect straight nose, and his lips had me curious to know how they would feel against mine and my body.

My eyes travel back up to a pair of eyes looking at me with a look of curiosity in them, and if possible. Sadness. For a moment I regretted asking him the question.

"We don't have to talk about it. If I get too personal, just let me know."

"It's not that." He responds coming to stand in front of me. "I actually would rather be doing something else right now." He responds in a huskier tone, while staring at my lips.

My breathing picks up a bit, and my heart is pounding in my chest.

Stepping in my personal space, he looks down at me and cups my face with his hands.

"What are you doing?" I ask him.

"This might sound crazy, but since meeting you. All I've wanted to do is kiss you." He says while rubbing one callous thumb against my lower lip.

"You expect me to let you kiss me after your mouth was all over Cassie's tonight?"

"She kissed me."

I lean in closer until my lips are less than an inch apart from his. "That may be but I didn't see you fighting her off either." My eyes linger to his lips. They were pink, full and kissable. I lick my own, then I pull away.

"What are you getting at Nyla?" He asks removing his hands from my face.

I look up at him then I shrug my shoulders.

"If I wanted to be with Cassie tonight. She would be the one standing here with me instead of you." He says somewhat in a cocky tone.

I raise my left eyebrow in question. Waiting on him to elaborate some more.

"When I left the club. I took her home. That's it. Then my plan was to drive back to the club and have a couple of drinks with the band, but of course that didn't happen."

I shake my head, and begin laughing to myself. "Mason. You don't owe me an explanation."

He stands there for a moment, not saying a word. Studying me like he's trying to solve a problem to a math equation.

"What's your story Nyla?"

"My story?"

"Like what's your favorite color. What kind of music do you listen to? What makes you happy, sad, or even cry?"

"Why?"

"What's wrong with me wanting to get to know you?"

"There's nothing wrong with it."

"Okay. Then what's your favorite color?"

"Yellow."

"What kind of music do you listen to?"

"Anything and everything good."

"What makes you happy, sad, or cry?"

"Why don't you stick around and find out." I respond with a hint of challenge.

"How long are you here for?"

"Two weeks. Is that plenty of time for you to complete my biography?"

"Smart ass." He says, showing off his gorgeous smile. "More than enough time." He says stepping back into my personal space again. "Just one kiss Nyla." He says changing the subject.

We stand there staring at each other in silence. Me staring at his lips, and him staring at mine. Then I allow the words to slip from my lips.

"Then kiss me."

nine
Mason

Then kiss me.

Is what she tells me. So I will. But if only she knew how bad I wanted to do so much more. Right now I wanted to peel this fuckin' dress off, so I could kiss, suck, lick, and bite every inch of her brown skin.

Putting my hands on the sides of her face again, I look down at a pair of lips that I so badly wanted to taste. They were thick and luscious. *I wonder how they would look wrapped around my dick?*

I lower my head until my lips are barely touching hers.

Nyla places her palms against my stomach and grabs a hold of my t-shirt, bunching it up between her fingers.

The feel of her tongue licking across my lower lip followed by her sucking my lip rings into her mouth causes me to fuckin' lose it.

When she releases my lip. I take the lead, and press my lips against hers, and we both moan into each other's mouths in unison.

Slipping my tongue between her lips I become lost and dizzy. Just one taste was all it took. I stumble forcing me forward, and pushing her against my car.

I was trying to take my time with her, as if she had a notice stamped on her body that said handle with care. From what I knew about her through Caleb, I knew she wasn't like one of the many women I've a been with that fucked me the first time they met me. But in the back of my mind, I wanted her to be that kind of girl for just one night. That's how bad I wanted her.

Placing my hands on her hips I push her further back on the car. Then I run my hands up and down her thighs, gently squeezing them. She voluntarily opens her legs to accommodate me. Deepening the kiss, I lean into her and bring her lower half closer to mine so she could feel how bad I wanted her.

She turns her head, pulling her lips away from mine. Placing a kiss to her cheek, I work my kisses down to her neck.

"Mason is that your phone ringing?"

Taking my lips away from her neck. I lift my head to listen. The muffled sound of my sister's ring tone was coming from my back pocket.

Groaning, I step away and turn my back to Nyla, I pull out my phone and answer.

"Brooke." I answer in a calm voice. "Whoa, calm down. What happened? Is she okay? I'm down the road I'll be there shortly."

I end my call and turn around and see Nyla on her feet, looking at me with concern on her face.

"Is everything alright?" She asks me.

"It's my grandma." I respond jogging to the driver side.

As soon as Nyla gets in and closes her door. I floor the gas petal and speed to my grandma's house. I pull up in front of the house and put my car in park. I hop out without taking the keys out the ignition or even taking the time to close the door. I run up the stairs and rush inside.

"Brooke!" I yell looking around the house.

"In here!" She yells back in response. I follow in the

direction from where her voice came, and I make my way to my grandma's room. As soon as I walk into her room, I hear the front door closing, totally forgetting that Nyla was with me.

My grandma was sitting up in her bed looking pale and exhausted, with Brooke by her side.

"What happened?"

"S-s-she started throwing up blood. I didn't know what to do." Brooke responds while trying to stop her own crying.

"Brooke, I think it's just a side effect from my new medicine. My Oncologist said it may cause nausea." My grandma responds in a weak voice, then starts coughing uncontrollably. She reaches over and grabs a tissue off her night stand and covers her mouth. When she's done, she looks up and looks over my shoulder. "I see we have a guest." She continues.

I turn around and see Nyla standing in the doorway.

"I'm sorry to intrude. I'll go wait for you in the living room." She says to me.

"Young lady wait. Mason who's this beautiful young lady that you left outside. Didn't I ever teach you any manners?" My grandma speaks up. Voice sounding stronger than before. "What's your name sweetheart?"

"Nyla."

"Well Nyla my name is Trisha, and as you probably already know I'm Mason's grandma and this young lady next to me is his younger sister Brooke."

"It's nice to meet both of you." Nyla responds.

"Well I wish it was in better terms. As you can see I'm a bit under the weather."

"I'm sorry that you're not feeling the best. I overheard you've been throwing up blood?" Nyla asked.

"Excuse me but I don't think it's any of your business. This is a family matter." Brooke says coming to her feet.

"Brooke." I say through gritted teeth.

"Stop you two!" My grandma interrupts while looking between the both of us. "Yes Nyla. I've been throwing up blood." She responds in a calm voice."

Nyla walks further into the room and takes a seat on my grandma's bed beside her. Surprising me and my sister.

Reaching her hand out, Nyla places her hand on my grandma's head. "What kind of medicine are you on?"

"So she thinks she's a fuckin' doctor now?" Brooke asks under her breath.

"Miss Trisha I'm not a doctor but I'm currently in school to become one." Nyla responds, answering Brooke's question indirectly. "Does your stomach hurt?"

"Nyla sweetheart. My whole body hurts."

I stand there watching my grandma share personal information with someone she didn't even know. *A complete stranger.*

"Again I'm not a doctor yet, but I do come from a family of doctors, and of course I pay attention in class." Nyla says.

Both she and my grandma share a laugh, causing my grandma to cough a little.

"But I think the medicine your Oncologist has recently put you on has upset your stomach. You could have a stomach ulcer or it could just be a new symptom you're experiencing from your treatments. All you can do right now is rest. Make an appointment with your doctor tomorrow to be on the safe side."

"I will do that Doctor Nyla." Grandma responds. "It was a pleasure meeting you young lady."

"Take care of yourself Trisha." Nyla responds.

Nyla stands and comes and stands beside me. "Your grandma could use some rest. If you want I can call a taxi to come and get me, so you don't have to leave."

"I'll be alright now will everyone please leave so I can rest." Grandma says in a sleepy voice.

Taking that as our cue. We leave my grandma alone to rest.

We make our way into the living room.

"I don't think my nerves can handle this Mason. I've never seen grandma this sick before." Brooke says plopping down on the worn out love seat. Looking exhausted.

"Like ma said. It's probably her new medicine." I say trying to figure out who I was trying to convince. The type of cancer she has and the stage she was in we knew she would possibly get worse.

"Brooke, why don't you go lay down and get some rest. With ma resting now, there's no reason for you to be up worrying, plus you have class tomorrow."

"Alright big bro I'm going." She responds with a yawn.

"I'm heading home. Call me if anything changes."

"Of course. And Nyla I'm sorry for how I acted in there."

"I'm sure I would have responded the same way." Nyla responds. Giving Brooke a gentle smile.

Brooke comes to her feet, and smiles in her direction. "Well good night you two. And Mason."

"Yeah?"

"You may want to keep her around." Brooke responds.

"Mind your business Brooke."

"I'm just saying." She says walking away.

Shaking my head to myself I turn my attention to Nyla.

"Are you ready?"

Nodding her head yes. We walk outside and get back into the car. The ride back to the house was quiet. Which I was grateful for because I really didn't want to discuss my grandma. Only a few people knew about my grandma's cancer, and I wanted to keep it that way. It was already tough enough having to respond to questions about how she was doing when I already knew deep down that she didn't have much time left to be with us. A year ago when she was diagnosed with lung cancer, the doctor told her that she would only have six months to live. Boy did she prove them wrong. That goes to show you that it's not all about what the doctors tell you. What it boils down to is that the Lord will call you when it's your time. I don't attend church every Sunday like I should, but I do know that there's a God, and when it's my grandma's time. She will go home to be with Him.

After about a fifteen-minute drive, I pull up into the driveway. I put Caleb's car in park, turn it off, and I get out and walk around to help Nyla out. Walking behind her, we make our way up to the front door. She looks through her purse and pulls out a key and opens the door. We step inside and as soon as the door closes she turns around and looks at me.

"Goodnight Mason, and thank you for taking me out

to your favorite spot. It was beautiful."

"You're welcome Nyla." I say looking down at her beautiful face.

She reaches into her purse and pulls out her phone. "What's your number?" She asks me.

After reciting my number to her. I stand there watching her type away on her phone.

"Got it. I'll text you in a few minutes so you can save my number." She says staring at my lips.

"Can I see you tomorrow?"

"We're living together now. Temporarily that is until I leave in two weeks, so I guess you will see me." She smiles.

"Good night Nyla."

Stepping forward, she stands on her tip toes and places her lips against mine. Pulling her head away, she steps back and turns around and walks down the hall to her room. She steps inside and turns around to glance at me one last time before closing the door behind her.

ten
Nyla

As soon as I close my door, I don't even cut the lights on. I place my purse on the bed and I remove my clothes. I walk over to the dresser and pull out an extra-large t-shirt and throw it on.

Pulling the covers back on my bed, I get in and pull the covers over my body. Grabbing my purse, I pull my phone out and I send a text to Caleb letting him know that I was home, then I send a quick one to Mason.

When I'm done, I place my phone and purse down on the night stand, I lay back against the pillow, and begin looking around my dark room at nothing in particular. My mind kept replaying tonight's events.

A light tapping noise on my door, interrupts my train of thought.

"Who is it?"

"Caleb."

"Come in." I say loud enough for him to hear.

He walks in and sits on my bed.

"So how was your night?" He asks me.

"Interesting." I respond.

"Would you mind going into more detail?"

"Why didn't you tell me that Mason's grandma had cancer?"

"It's not my place to tell. What all did he tell you?"

"Not much. I accidentally found out, and then the mention of his grandma having an Oncologist was all I needed to know."

"Did he tell you what kind of cancer?"

"No." I say shaking my head. "It's bad enough she has it. I'm not going to ask him either. I can tell by looking at him that he's having a real tough time." I pause for a minute, when another question comes to mind. "Does he have any other family members in the area?"

"Nyla it's not..."

"I know your position to tell? Come on Caleb!"

"This is between you and me. Do you understand?"

"Yes! Now would you tell me already!"

"Well he knows nothing about his dad, and his mom is currently serving a twenty-year jail sentence for possession of drugs and attempted murder."

"Twenty years?"

"Yeah. Could have been longer, but she took a plea deal. She's been in and out of prison since Mason was six. Eventually DHR stepped in and his grandma was awarded custody. She adopted both him and his sister and has been raising them ever since. So you can imagine what he's going through. His grandma and sister mean the world to him. Sometimes you may hear him refer to his grandma as ma."

"I really hate to see him and his sister go through this. I wish there was more I could do for them. I know I just met him, but I wouldn't wish this on anyone."

"I know Nyla. That's why I know you're going to be an awesome doctor. You've always been the caring type."

"Thanks Caleb."

"Yeah, yeah." He laughs. "Well thanks for texting me to let me know you made it home. I have a pretty thang waiting on me back in my room so I'm going to leave you so you can get some rest." He says standing up from my bed. "Oh I'm having a couple of people over for a barbecue tomorrow night. Did you want to catch a movie before then?"

"Sure. That would be nice."

"Alright. Well good night big head."

I grab a pillow off my bed and I throw it in his direction, only to miss when he darts out the door and closing it behind him.

I lay back down, and my phone chirps alerting me that I have a text message. I grab it off the night stand, and I see a text from Mason.

Mason: I can't sleep.

I can only imagine. I think to myself before responding.

Nyla: Me either.

I lied.

Mason: How about we help each other out?

Nyla: What do you have in mind?

Mason: You'll see...

What did he mean by that?

Nyla: Mason?

Mason: I'm on my way to your room.

He's what!

I scramble out of my bed and rush into my bathroom to make sure I looked presentable. I'm running my hands through my hair when I hear my phone beep.

Mason: I'm outside your door.

Nyla: Come in.

I leave my bathroom just in time to see Mason's figure walking across my room. I walk over to the small desk in the corner to cut the light on, and see Mason standing there in a pair of gray cotton pajama pants and a black t-shirt.

"Hey." He says in a low voice.

"Hey. Have you checked on your grandma?"

"Yeah. Brooke said she's still asleep."

"Good. I'm glad she's resting well."

We stand there in silence not knowing what to do next.

"Mason why are you here?"

Before responding. I watch as his eyes trail over the length of my body. He was looking at me in a way that should make me feel uncomfortable, but instead it made me feel sexy as hell.

Lifting his eyes to mine, he walks over to me and tugs at the hem of my t-shirt. "I love this look on you." He says with a sexy smirk on his face.

Damn he's dangerous.

"I thought we both agreed we would help each other

get some sleep?" He continues.

"Actually you didn't give me a chance to agree, but that's fine. We can talk some more if you want."

I walk around him and make my way back to my bed. I get in and slide under the covers.

With that same sexy ass smirk on his face, he removes his shirt, cuts my lamp off and joins me in my bed.

"Then let's talk." He responds.

He fluffs up two pillows, then lays on his side looking at me.

"So you want to be a doctor?" He asks me.

"That's my plan." I respond with a yawn.

"Doctor Nyla." He says my name making it sound like the sexiest thing ever.

"So who in your family is in the medical field?"

"My mom." I pause letting another yawn take over. "Is an Emergency Room Nurse, my aunt is an Ob-Gyn Doctor, my uncle is a Nurse Practitioner, and my grandfather was a

ER Doctor. So it kind of runs in my family." I finish my sentence sounding exhausted.

"How many years of school do you have left?"

I close my eyes, thinking over his answer. "About nine and a half years." My voice drifts out in a lazy and sleepy sound.

Mason doesn't say anything else. There was nothing but silence between us. I snuggle my head deeper into my pillow, and I pull the covers up higher on my body.

The bed shifts a little and I feel Mason's hand on my hip. I turn on my back and to my other side facing away from him. His hand comes around to my stomach and he pulls me back until my body molds against his.

"Good night Mason." I whisper.

He kisses the back of my head, and I fall asleep.

eleven
Nyla

I wake up the next morning to an empty bed. I glance at the alarm clock on the night stand and notice that I was up earlier than normal considering I had nowhere to be until that afternoon. After several failed attempts of trying to go back to sleep I get up and start unpacking several other items I didn't get to yesterday. After a long shower, I get dressed and decide to go for a ride. I grab the spare keys to Caleb's car, and I send him a text letting him know I had his car.

I'm driving and trying my best to go by memory alone, since it was dark when Mason traveled down this street. I eventually slow down and turn off onto the familiar dirt road. I keep straight and continue my way down then I make a slight right and I keep driving until Mason's grandma's house comes into view. I pull up into the yard and park beside Mason's car. I cut the engine and I sit there for a minute realizing that it was possible that his grandma wasn't home. I get out and I look around the yard and I start walking around the house where I would hopefully find Mason.

A small white barn that could use a paint job comes

into view. The large wooden doors were wide open and the sound of blues music could be heard. An older model Honda sat in the space with its hood popped up. As I get closer I can see Mason's shirtless form working underneath it. He had on a pair of old ripped jeans, work boots, and he had areas on his body that were covered in oil and sweat.

"Shit!" He yells. The rag he had in his hand was thrown to the ground. He looks up and sees he has an audience now. "Nyla?"

"Hey." I walk around to get a better view of what he was working on. "I see you got your tire fixed."

"Yeah a buddy of mine hooked my car up to his truck and brought it here for me. I just finished replacing the tire." He responds.

"So this must be your sister's car. Do you need any help?"

He stands there looking at the sundress I had on before answering me. "You probably should take that dress off. I would hate to see what a little oil and sweat will do to it."

"I think I'll keep it on."

"Just know I gave you a fair warning. If anything gets on that cute little dress of yours. It's not my fault." With one more quick perusal of my body he turns his attention back to his task at hand. Giving me a back view of his body.

My eyes trail over the muscles in his back and arms, and I watch as they tighten with every movement.

"So what brings you here? Did you miss me that much that you couldn't wait until I got back?"

I couldn't help the laugh that slips from my mouth.

"Actually I wanted to see how your grandma was feeling. Is she home?"

He turns his head and looks over his shoulder at me. He looks at me for several quiet moments before turning around again to his work. "She's inside getting her rest. Doc prescribed some more medication and told her she needs to stay in bed."

"Did they say anything else?"

"If they did she didn't tell me. Can you pass me that flash light and wrench that's behind you on that table?"

I turn around and grab both items off the table and I

hand them to him.

"So what's the problem?" I ask referring to the car.

"Nothing. Now that I've fixed it. I'm changing the oil now and I'm just making sure everything else looks fine."

"Do you have a lot of other jobs lined up?"

"Not really. I've turned a lot of jobs down. Most of my time has been spent with the band, since we have the tour coming up."

"So when you're not working. How are you..."

"What paying the bills?" He asks with irritation in his voice.

"I didn't mean it like that. You told me that you support your grandma and sister. I know it has to be tough."

"What do you know about struggling? I bet your parents get you anything you want. Including that dress you have on."

"I'm not some rich girl that gets whatever she wants. Yes, my parents have money but that doesn't mean I see a dime of it! Matter of fact I've worked my ass off to get the scholarships I've earned to put me through to the school of my choice. The day I told my parents that I didn't want to go to their alma mater. They told me I would have to figure out a way to pay for it. So I did."

"And what does that have to do with struggling? Huh?"

"You know what? Fuck you Mason! I'm leaving. I have plans with Caleb anyway."

"Well I hope you're going home to change first."

"What's wrong with what I have on?"

"It's dirty." He responds.

I look down at my dress confused to what he was talking about. I look up in time to see Mason walking in my direction. "Don't you even think about it."

"What?" He asks all innocent.

"Stay away from me Mason."

I turn around to make a run for it, but I don't get too far. Mason grabs my wrist, turns me around to face him and pulls me against his body. "I think you knew exactly what you were doing showing up in this dress. Especially when you know how bad I wanted to fuck you last night." He says into my ear, then he lowers his head and kisses the side of my neck. "How about we stop playing these games and give each other what we both want. Hmm? I promise you'll like it." He whispers against my skin.

The sound of someone clearing their throat catches our attention.

"Hey Nyla. Mason. I'm sorry to interrupt your little fuck fest but I was wondering Mason if you were done with my car? I have my last class of the day in two hours."

Mason pulls away from my neck and I turn around and see his sister Brooke standing there with a smirk on her face. I pry myself away from Mason and I turn around and run my hands down my dress.

"If you would like Nyla. I can give you the number to my cleaners?" Brooke says while looking at my dress that was now covered in oil and Mason's sweat. I look up at him and see him smiling down at me.

"I told you to take it off." He says.

"Jack ass." I mumble under my breath. I turn around and make my way out the garage. "Brooke please let your grandma know that I came by to see how she was doing." I say over my shoulder and continue across the yard.

"Nyla!" I can hear Mason shout my name. I stop and turn around.

"I'm sorry." He says with a smile on his face.

"This isn't funny Mason. This isn't coming out!"

"I'll buy you another one." He says placing both of his hands on my hips. "You can't show up here looking this sexy and expect me to keep my hands to myself. He grabs my right hand and places it over the front of his jeans. "Do you feel how bad I want you right now?" He lowers his head and kisses me on my lips. "I'm sorry for what I said back there. Let me make it up to you." He says against my lips before sliding his tongue between my lips. Wrapping his arms around my waist he pulls me tighter against his body and squeezes my ass in the process.

I tear my lips away and create space between us. "I have to go."

"Are you sure you don't want me to come with you. I can help you with your dress." He says then winks at me.

"No. I'll manage." I turn around and walk to the car.

"Nyla!" I hear Mason call out my name again.

"Bye Mason." I call over my shoulder.

I lower myself into Caleb's car and I look ahead and see Mason still standing there. I cut the car on and I put it in reverse. With a honk to the horn, I put the car in drive and I make my way back to the main road.

twelve
Nyla

"How many people did you invite over Caleb?" I ask while getting out his car. We just got home from the movies to find cars lined up and down the street and scattered in his front yard.

"Enough." He responds with a smile on his face. "But that's the joys of having a house on a street with very few neighbors where you don't have to worry about anyone complaining about parties, noise, and the amount of company you have over."

I shake my head and slide the spaghetti strap of my yellow romper that crisscrossed in the back up my shoulders. It was so hot that I was glad that I decided to pull my hair up into a top knot, giving more of a view of my exposed shoulders and back. I make my way up the sidewalk to the front door. Before I could open the door, Jax swings the door open.

"It's about time you got here."

"Hey Jax." I respond walking inside.

"How was the movie?" He asks me.

"Boring. Caleb fell asleep."

"I was resting my eyes." Caleb says behind me.

"Whatever." I say, rolling my eyes.

"Sounds like something Caleb would do." Jax laughs. "Well everyone is out back. Can I get you guys something to drink? We have beer, soda, and water."

"I'll take a water please."

"I'm good." Caleb responds.

"Okay go out back and get comfortable, I'll grab your water Nyla and meet you out there."

"Thanks Jax."

He winks at me and walks off.

Caleb and I walk through a set of doors leading out to his backyard. Tiki lights were lit throughout the yard, and several lanterns were hung up illuminating the area. People were in the pool, and some were sitting around talking. I look around and I spot Evan and Jeremy behind the grill.

We make our way around the pool, and my attention is drawn to Mason, who's talking to a group of people inside the pool.

"Nyla!" Jeremy shouts bringing everyone's attention to him.

"Hey you guys."

"Sup Nyla. Caleb" Evan speaks.

I wave and Caleb nods in his direction.

"You two hungry?" Jeremy asks.

"I'm not hungry, I think I ate too much popcorn."

"Okay, well there's plenty of food. Can I get you something Caleb?"

"Yeah man I'll take two burgers."

"Two burgers coming up." Jeremy responds.

"I see you've caught the attention of Mason. He's making his way over as we speak." Caleb says to me. He grabs his plate from Jeremy and begins walking towards the house. "I'll catch you later Nyla." He says over his shoulder.

"Okay." I respond.

I take a deep breath and continue to watch Evan flip burgers on the grill when I feel drops of water hit my shoulders, then the gentle touch of someone's lips against my neck.

I turn around and there he was dripping wet from head to toe. My eyes wander over his body and landing on his nipple rings.

"Hey." I say unable to take my eyes off of him.

"I'm heading inside, you wanna come with me?"

"Sure."

Surprising me, he reaches out and grabs my hand and leads me through the backyard and into the house. Every once and awhile, we would get stopped because someone wanted to talk to him. We walk across the house and down the short hallway and into a room.

"This is my room." He says cutting on the light switch. "Make yourself at home. I'm going to shower real quick."

He shuts his bedroom door and locks it, and makes his way into the attached bathroom, closing the door behind him. At the sound of the shower coming on, I decide to look around his room. The first thing that I noticed was the huge bookshelf that covered half his wall. I walk over and notice the books were mostly Non Fiction, Biographies, and books about music. I turn around and examine the rest of his room. His walls were painted a dark gray and posters of music icons were scattered across them. Several guitars sat on stands in the corner of his room near an oversized chaise arm chair, and his bed was large but simple, with a black headboard, and covered in a black and blue comforter. A large TV was mounted on the wall on the opposite wall with a small shelf underneath that stored his DVD collection. I walk over and kneel down to look at his collection, and smile when I see a lot of movies that were my favorites.

I hear the shower shut off, but continue to browse his collection. Seeing one that I haven't seen in a while, I pick it up and start reading the description on the back when the door to the bathroom opens. Mason steps out still damp, with a towel hanging off his narrow hips, towel drying his hair.

"Why do you have so many books?" I ask the first question that comes to my mind.

He tosses the towel he was using to dry his hair, to the floor and walks over to his closet and pulls out some clothes, then he walks in my direction to a dresser that was sitting against the wall, and pulls out a pair of boxers.

I stand there awaiting my answer, wondering if he even heard me. Coming to stand in front of me he takes the DVD out my hands and looks at it.

"We should watch this together sometime." He smiles and hands it back to me. He taps my chin with his finger, bringing my full attention to his face. "And the answer to your question. I love to read. A lot." He says after a brief pause, while looking at my lips. Making me feel as if he was insinuating something else. "Do you?"

"I use to until college happened. My major requires me to read a lot."

"Well it's too bad that you don't love to read. I heard it helps relax the mind and body." He winks at me.

He turns around, and walks back into the bathroom, closing the door but not all the way this time.

I put the DVD back and walk over to his night stand beside his bed, that has several pictures on it. Looking over them I come across a picture of Mason, Brooke, and his grandma. The next one was of him and the band, and the last one was a black and white photo of him laughing while posing on a stool shirtless. I pick it up unable to tear my gaze away.

I hear the door to the bathroom open and Mason walks out in a pair of khaki cargo shorts, and a light blue t-shirt.

"I've got to go down in the basement and grab some pieces of music Caleb and I have been working on. Did you want to stay in here and wait for me or did you want to go down with me?"

"I'll go with you."

"Cool. Let's go." He says holding his hand out.

I sit the photo down, and I reach for Mason's outstretched hand.

He unlocks his bedroom door and opens it to find Cassie standing on the other side with a smile on her face until she sees me standing there.

"What the fuck is going on? What is this bitch doing in here?" She asks, while glaring me up and down.

"Cassie calm down." Mason says through gritted teeth. "What are you doing here?" He asks while squeezing my hand.

"I thought I was invited." She responds still glaring at me. "Did you just fuck her?" She asks giving her attention to Mason now.

Before I could respond, Mason cuts in. "Nyla can you give me five minutes?"

Pulling my hand away from his, I walk around Cassie, staring her down, walking into the hallway. Just in time to hear the door slam behind me.

I make my way to the kitchen where I find Caleb talking to Jax. When they see me. They stop their conversation.

"I was just looking for you." Caleb says. "Where have you been?"

Before I can answer, the sound of Cassie's voice catches our attention. We turn around and see Cassie storming through the kitchen and to the front door.

"You can lose my fuckin' number Mason!" She yells over her shoulder. With a final glare in my direction, she walks out the front door, slamming it behind her.

"What the fuck was that about?" I hear Jax say.

"There's no telling with her." Caleb says. "Maybe that one will get a clue and see that Mason isn't interested in her ass anymore."

"That boy sure can pick them." I hear Jax snicker.

I tear my eyes away from the closed front door, and back to Jax and Caleb, when I see Mason walk in.

"Nyla, what were you saying?" Caleb asks me.

Before I can respond, Mason walks over and stands close behind me, and places one hand to my hip. He leans in, and his lips brush against my ear.

"Nyla can we talk?" He whispers in my ear.

With a slight nod, I turn around and come face to face with him. He steps away giving me some space, then he turns around and walks over to the basement door and opens it and stands there waiting on me.

I glance at Caleb who's looking at me wondering what the hell is going on.

Ignoring his questioning stare, I follow Mason.

We walk down the steps leading into the basement.

"Is she your girlfriend?" I ask him.

"Don't you think it's a little late that you're asking me that?"

"Well is she?"

"No she's not my girlfriend Nyla."

"Then what is she to you? Why did she act like that?" I ask coming to stand in front of him.

He stands there looking down at me, trying to figure out the best way to explain the situation better.
"Cassie is someone I use to fuck." He continues. Stepping closer to me. "Does that bother you?"

"Why would it bother me?"

"Well if you haven't already guessed it. I want you Nyla."

"What if I have a boyfriend?"

"Do you?" He asks coming much closer to me.

"No." I say breathless.

"Then what's the problem Nyla? You let me kiss you, and let's not forget. You let me hold you all night long."

"True. Then I woke up alone."

"Only because I had to get up early and take my grandma to her doctor's appointment. I want you so fuckin' bad that it hurts Nyla." He says closing the space between us, not leaving any room. "Let me show you just how bad." He continues.

Grabbing me by my hips, he lowers his head and begins placing kisses along my neck.

"Mason." I moan out.

"Nyla." He says against my neck, while working his way up, and placing kisses along my jawline. Gently grabbing my face, he places a kiss to my chin, then nibbles on my lower lip and sucks it into his mouth, before kissing and tasting every inch of my mouth. The way he was kissing me, had me wishing his mouth was somewhere else on my body. *Damn he could kiss.*

129

"Yo Mason, are you down there!"

The sound of his name being yelled from the top of the stairs, has me pulling my lips away from his.

"Don't stop. They'll go away." He whispers against my lips, before capturing my mouth in a kiss again.

The sound of footsteps making their way down the stairs has me pushing him away, and creating space between us. I look up the stairs and find Jeremy making his way down.

"Hey man. I'm sorry to bother you, but everyone wants to know if you could sing a little something?" Jeremy asks.

Still feeling his gaze on me, he answers. "Yeah can you give me a minute?"

"No problem man." With one final look at us, Jeremy runs back upstairs.

I turn my head and make eye contact with Mason. "Well I guess you should head on up. You don't want to keep them waiting."

"Stay with me tonight." He says walking to me. He

places a kiss to my forehead and tilts my head back and kisses my lips. "In my bed." He whispers against my lips.

"Shouldn't we slow down?"

"No, but I'll go as slow as you want me to Nyla."

"I'm serious Mason."

"I'm serious too." He responds.

"Mason are you coming?" Jeremy yells his name again.

"Shit." He says to himself. "Yeah!" He yells back.

He grabs my hand and places a kiss on the back of it, then he begins making his way up the stairs, pulling me with him.

We make our way outside where everyone is gathered around a fire pit. All eyes are on us as soon as we walk over.

Mason comes to a stop and turns around and looks down at me. "I'm serious about what I said. I want you with me tonight."

"Okay."

He smiles and walks away and sits with the band.

I look around and find Sierra waving in my direction. I walk around several people and take a seat beside her.

"So what have you two been up to?" She asks wiggling her eyebrows at me.

I smile, politely ignoring her question, and I look up and my eyes instantly lock with Mason's.

He's just sitting there with the rest of the band, staring at me with his guitar in his hands.

"I want to thank everyone for coming out tonight. It's pretty late so I'm going to sing one song tonight. This song was written by Caleb's dad several years ago and it's called Beautiful, and I hope you like it."

I watch as his fingers dance along the strings creating yet another hypnotic melody. He closes his eyes and parts his lips, and the sweetest sound escapes. I sit there blocking out everyone around me, keeping all my attention on him. My eyes linger to his mouth watching the way his lips formed the intoxicating words that were making their debut.

"Damn why does he have to be so talented." I hear

Sierra say beside me.

I close my eyes and begin swaying back and forth, getting lost in the lyrics. The words were beautiful, just like the title of the song. He was talking about getting lost in someone and being in love. The lyrics stop and the sound of his guitar continues to play on. Eventually slowing down and coming to a stop. Followed by the sound of applause.

I open my eyes and look around and see everyone clapping.

"Thank you and I hope everyone had a good time. Good night."

He stands and removes the guitar strap from around his neck and passes it to Evan, then stops and talks to Jess, who was dying to get his attention. He politely acknowledges her, then makes his way to me.

He gives Sierra a hug, and she starts whispering in his ear. He laughs out and they pull away from each other.

"You two have a good night." She says winking in my direction. "Mason remember what I said."

He shakes his head and smiles. "Okay Sierra."

"Bye you two."

As soon as she walks off, Mason's attention is back on me. He wraps his arm around my shoulder, hugging me close to his body, and I wrap my arm around his waist.

We walk into the house and through a crowd of people, trying to make their way out the front door. Finally, we make it back to his room. He cuts on the lamp sitting on his night stand and makes his way to his dresser, and pulls out a t-shirt.

"Here's something for you to sleep in. I'm going to help get everyone cleared out, and I'll be right back.

"Okay."

He stares at me for several seconds, then walks out the door closing it behind him.

I slide the straps of my romper off my shoulders, letting the fabric fall to the floor. I pick it up and place it on his desk chair, before slipping Mason's shirt over my body. I release my hair from my top knot, and I grab the remote off his night stand and I cut the TV on. I flip through a couple of channels, stopping on a movie channel. I toss the remote on the bed, and I make my way over to his book shelf. I reach up and pull a book off. I open it and start flipping through the pages.

The door opens and Mason walks in and locks it behind him.

"I thought you didn't like reading." He says walking in my direction.

"Mason..."

Before I could finish my sentence. His lips were on mine. Possessing my mouth and shutting me up. The book that I held in my hand, falls to the floor. Totally forgotten.

"Let's play a game." He says against my lips. "It's called Can I. The rules are simple Nyla. I'll ask if I can do something for you, and your response must be yes or no. That's it. Do you understand?"

"Yes." I respond.

"First question." He pauses to place a kiss against my lips. Can I please you with my mouth?"

"What do you mean by..."

"Nyla. Yes, or no." He interrupts me. "If it makes you

feel any better. I promise I won't hurt you. Nothing but pleasure." He says nibbling on my lower lip.

"Mason."

"Nyla." He says in warning.

"Yes." I respond right before his tongue enters into my mouth.

thirteen
Mason

Why couldn't I get enough of her when I haven't even fucked her yet?

I withdraw my tongue and begin tasting her lips.

"I can't stop thinking about you Nyla." I confess pulling my mouth away from hers.

"You know nothing about me Mason."

"I know your favorite color is yellow, you love all kinds of music, and the rest I'll just have to learn and figure out."

With my hands resting on her hips. I run my hands to the small of her back and down to her ass, pulling her closer to my body. Lowering my head, I press my lips to the side of her neck, and I part my lips so my tongue could taste her skin.

"I can't wait to taste the rest of your body." I whisper against her skin.

Sliding my hands up from her ass. My hands wander underneath her shirt, making contact with her warm, smooth brown skin of her back. They continue to slide up her back, reaching her shoulder blades, then back down to cuff her perfect ass.

Lifting my head away from her neck. I place a peck to her lips before grabbing the hem of her shirt.

"Can I take your shirt off?" I ask already lifting it up her body.

"Yes." She responds with hooded eyes.

She raises her arms above her head and allows me to pull the shirt completely off of her. Tossing the shirt aside, my eyes land on a perfect set of breasts, with nipples that I'm going to refer to as Hershey Kisses. The rest of her body was toned and curvy in all the right places.

I reach out and touch both of her nipples with the pads of my thumbs, and the most erotic moan slips from her lips. She responded well to my touch. Just the thought of hearing her moan my name caused my erection to grow harder.

Grabbing the hem of my shirt I pull it over my head, letting it fall to the floor.

I watch as Nyla's eyes travel over my upper body appreciating every tattoo, muscle, and piercing her eyes came in contact with.

I reach out and pull her against my body. It felt so good having her breast pressed against my bare chest.

Bending slightly at the knees, I wrap my arms around her waist and start sucking on the side of her neck. Everywhere my mouth touched, I could physically feel her shiver in my arms.

"Are you okay?" I ask, now trailing kisses up her neck.

"Yes." She moans her response.

"If I do something that doesn't feel right, or if I hurt you in any way, I want you to let me know. Okay?" I whisper in her ear.

"Yes." She responds.

"Good." I whisper back. I suck her earlobe into my mouth, then I tug it gently with my teeth before releasing it.

Turning her around until her back is pressed against my chest. I pull her hair up and away from her neck, and I reach around and grab both breasts with my hands while placing kisses along the nape of her neck, working my way down her back, kissing each shoulder blade, before trailing down until I reach the small dimples in her back.

Reaching for the fabric of her bikini underwear I tug on them, pulling them down slowly over her shapely hips, and over her thighs until they reach her ankles. Lifting each foot off the floor, I help her step out of them, leaving them on the floor. I turn her around once again, and start kissing my way up.

fourteen
Nyla

Mason kisses my left knee, then nibbles and bites his way up my thigh. Leaning forward he places a kiss on my pelvic bone, kisses his way to my belly button and up until he reaches my breasts.

A soft moan escapes my lips, and I begin to feel weak in the knees. Mason hugs me against his body, holding me tight so I wouldn't fall. When he comes to a standing position, I run my hands through his dark silky strands. He looks down at me with gray eyes that are usually light in color, but now looked dark and dangerous.

Pulling his head down to mine. My lips touch his, kissing him hard. Tugging at his strands he moans into my mouth, before lifting me off the floor. I wrap my legs around him, tightening my arms and legs around him, holding on tight as we make our way over to his bed.

With a groan, Mason pulls his lips away from mine, to concentrate on where he's going.

"I can't have us bumping into shit." He says with a laugh.

"Please don't." I respond against his neck, where I start a combination of sucks and kisses.

"You're driving me crazy Nyla." He moans.

When his legs come in contact with the bed we fall on top of it. Mason dips his tongue inside my mouth, wasting no time. Sucking on my lips he lifts his head and looks down at me, and slowly unwraps my legs from around him. He stands, and removes a foil packet from his cargo shorts, and tosses it on the bed. He removes his shorts and stands there in only his boxers.

Sitting up, I come to my knees and move closer to Mason. He was so fuckin' sexy. My eyes travel from his lips down to his neck where his skin was decorated in ink in all shapes, sizes and colors all the way to the top of his boxers. His tats covered a majority of his body, but I was unsure of what lied beneath his boxers. Leaning forward I suck his right pierced nipple into my mouth, releasing it and swirling my tongue around it, causing him to hiss.

I come to a sitting position and I reach for the elastic band of his boxers.

"Can I?"

"Yes." He responds through gritted teeth.

I tug and slide his boxers off his lean hips.

Reaching out I begin stroking him, loving the way his erect dick felt in my hand. He was perfect. Not too big, and definitely not small. He had nothing to be ashamed of.

I grip a little tighter, causing a hissing moan to slip from his lips again.

He tilts his head back and closes his eyes.

"Shit please don't stop." He responds with a tortured moan.

He slowly opens his eyes and stares down at me, focusing all of his attention on my mouth.

Looking up into his eyes, I lean forward and circle my tongue around his tip before sucking it into my mouth. Working my mouth around his tip, I begin sucking more of him into my mouth until I can't fit no more in. Relaxing a little, I open my mouth wider, taking more of him in.

"Nyla." He says in a breathless moan. "Fuck that feels so good."

He runs his hand through my strands, gathering some of it in his hand, gripping it gently, guiding my head up and down his dick.

A moan slips from my lips, and I begin sucking harder wanting to taste more of him. I couldn't get enough, I was becoming addicted, I couldn't stop so I continued tasting every inch of him.

Mason tugs on my hair, pulling my mouth away.

I look up at him, with a confused expression on my face, wondering why he stopped me.

He leans down and attacks my mouth, and our mouths begin to battle. It was more of a fight to see how much of each other we could taste. It was pure desperation.

Pushing my body back down on the bed. He moves over my body, and settles between my legs again allowing me to feel his bare erection between my legs.

He flicks his tongue across my lips, before kissing me deeply again. He releases my lips, and kisses my chin, moving lower to my neck, between my breasts, and down to my stomach.

Spreading my legs wide with his hands, he leans down

and places a kiss to the outer lips of my pussy.

"Open it for me." He says in a husky demand. "I want you to hold it open for me until I'm done tasting every inch of your pretty pussy."

I do as I'm told, and I spread my lower lips with my fingers. Giving him a view of my aroused treasure.

He brushes his thumb over my clit. Causing me to arch my back off the bed, and moaning out his name.

"Relax Nyla."

Lowering his head, he gently sucks my clit into his mouth.

"Mmm." He moans.

He releases it, and sucks it back into his mouth. Repeating this torturous move several times.

I lay there with my legs spread wide open, trying to keep myself open to him, while enjoying the way he took his time licking, kissing, and sucking a part of me that no one's ever really took the time to explore.

Trust me. I'm not a virgin. My friend Jordyn was the

only one who knew about my lack of sexual experience. As far as being with only one person. I told her everything when it came to my nonexistent sex life. At one point I thought there was something wrong with me, but she convinced me that the guy I was seeing at that time in my life, was an asshole and was more concerned about pleasing himself and could care less if I was getting anything out of it.

As soon as I feel his tongue slide inside of me, I lose it. I close my eyes and a scream leaves my mouth, while my body starts shaking voluntarily on its own.

I lay there relaxed and in a daze, while Mason continues savoring every inch of me.

He lifts his head and licks his lips, and crawls his way up my body until we're face to face.

Reaching over, he grabs the condom, then lowers his head and begins kissing me deeply. Giving me a sample of how I tasted off his lips.

"Are you tired? I can stop." He asks against my lips. He lifts his head and looks down at me. He pushes several strands of my hair away from my face waiting on me to answer him.

"I'm fine. Please don't stop."

Sliding off the bed he comes to a standing position and grabs a hold of my ankles and pulls me down.

"Good. Turn over."

I turn over giving him a perfect view of my ass. I can hear the crinkle and opening of the foil condom wrapper behind me. I look over my shoulder and watch him roll the condom over his erection.

When he's done. He places a number of kisses along the arch of my back, and puts his hands on my hips. I lift up until I'm on all fours. He grips my hip with one hand, and positions himself at my entrance. In a slow torturous move he enters me.

"Nyla." He moans out my name in satisfaction.

Gripping my hips tightly he continues to slowly move his way inside me.

Tugging on my hair with his free hand, he pulls his hips away, and enters me with one big thrust. The mixture of both pain and pleasure consumes my body, and for the umpteenth time that night his name slips from my lips.

I close my eyes slowly, and I start moaning in

satisfaction, enjoying the way he was working my body from behind.

Damn he felt good.

"Shit Nyla. I'm thinking about fucking you all night. Do you think you can handle me?" He asks moving deeper inside of me.

I scream out, calling his name once again.

He lowers his head and bites my shoulder then soothes it with his tongue.

"I really enjoyed seeing your lips wrapped around my dick tonight." He whispers in my ear.

"Aaaaaah." I scream out. Coming for the hundredth time that night...Ever.

"Nyla I want to hear you scream my name one more time and I promise we'll get some sleep."

"Mason please." I whisper. Feeling so exhausted.

"Baby I promise. Just one more time and I'll stop. I'm sorry but I can't help that you feel so fuckin' good."

I reach behind me and run my fingers through his hair. Turning my head to face him, my tongue glides into his mouth enjoying the mixture of him and myself on his tongue. I lower my head to the bed, bringing him with me, and I begin to slowly rotate my hips. He groans, and begins to move faster and deeper inside of me, than I thought possible. He releases my lips and lowers his head to the side of my neck.

"Shit!" He shouts, releasing himself into the condom.

He lays on top of me for several seconds before slowly removing himself from me. He gets out of bed and walks into the bathroom to dispose the condom.

I lay there on my side, tired and barely able to keep my eyes open. He walks out the bathroom and my eyes roam over his naked body, landing on his erection, that showed signs of being ready for another round.

The bed dips behind me, and Mason runs his hand down the length of my back, before spooning me against his warm body. Holding me tight.

I close my eyes, and relax against him. Loving the way my body molded against his warm, hard, and sweaty body. It felt so good.

With the warmth of his body against mine. I yawn one final time before falling into a deep blissful sleep.

fifteen
Mason

The ring tone that I have assigned for Jax, starts ringing, filling my room with the soft rock melody from one of my favorite bands. Instinctively I pull Nyla's body closer to mine, not wanting to wake up. Hell I would stay in bed the rest of the day, if it meant having her with me.

My phone stops ringing, and Nyla starts to shift in my arms. Just the slight wiggle of her ass against my dick, had me moaning and tightening my hold around her stomach.

"Good morning." She says yawning, and turning on her back in my arms.

My eyes roam over her naked body, that was currently uncovered. After we fucked, we got so hot that we didn't even need a blanket to keep us warm from the cool air coming from the AC, but just our body temperature alone was enough.

I wouldn't mind having an instant replay from last night, but before I could make my move, my phone starts ringing again.

"You should get that. It must be important if they're calling you a second time this morning."

She sits up and pecks me on the lips.

"I'm going to shower real quick."

I watch her climb out of my bed, keeping my eyes on the sway of her hips as she walks into the bathroom.

With a groan, I get out of bed and walk over to my cargo shorts that were laying on the floor. Picking them up I reach inside and retrieve my phone. Once again my phone stops ringing again. I enter my passcode and I call Jax back.

After three rings he answers.

"Where the fuck are you?"

"I'm just waking up. What's up?"

"Man we've been sitting in this studio waiting on your ass for the last thirty minutes."

"Fuck! Man I'm so sorry. It slipped my mind. Give me fifteen minutes and I'll be there."

"Look man I know you've had a lot going on lately

okay. Just be careful and bring yo ass!" Jax says into the phone before disconnecting the call.

I toss my phone on the bed, and I walk into the bathroom and see Nyla's silhouette through the steamed up glass shower door.

I walk quietly over to the shower door and I slide it open and step inside, sliding it behind me. I stand there in silence, watching the water slide down the length of her body.

I walk closer and I place my hands along her back, and immediately I feel her muscles tense under my touch. I run my hands up and down, before leaning down to place gentle kisses against her shoulder blades.

"Mason." She moans my name. "Is everything okay?"

"Everything is fine. It was Jax. I forgot we had rehearsals today, so now he's pissed."

She slowly turns around and leans her back against the shower tile.

My eyes lock with hers for a moment before they travel down to her nose, lips, breasts, stomach, and the spot between her legs.

"You're so beautiful." I say while stepping closer. Gently placing my hands on the sides of her cheeks, I lower my head and kiss the lips I've been dying to kiss all morning.

"Mason. Stop. You better hurry up and get going."

"Why? Don't you want my kisses?"

"Of course." She responds.

I grab some of my body wash and begin lathering up my body.

"Nyla, last night was amazing." I stare into her eyes so she could see how serious I was. "I don't know what you've heard about me, but I don't want you to think this is just about sex."

"Mason."

"We can talk about this later. But I thought you should know."

She stands there for a moment just staring up at me. "But what if I want to talk about it now?" She asks in a teasing voice.

She reaches between my legs and begins stroking me.

"Nyla." I say in warning through gritted teeth.

Standing on her tip toes, she presses her lips against mine. Pulling away she runs her tongue across my bottom lip, before sucking it into her mouth. Releasing my lip, she kisses my chin, and works her way down to my neck, then my chest. Stopping to circling her tongue around my left pierced nipple, then she pulls away from me.

"We will talk about this later Mason." She says turning away from me.

"Wait a minute. Where are you going?" I asked aroused and pissed at the same time.

"Remember it's not about the sex right?" She winks at me before leaving the shower.

* * *

After fifteen minutes of getting my ass chewed out by my band mates and two hours of practice. I turn onto the road, to a place I called home for past couple of years of my life. As I get closer I see an ambulance with its flashing lights on, parked in the yard. I increase my speed and park my car. I

155

get out and look around and I don't see my sister's car anywhere. Which means my grandma was home by herself. I jog up the stairs, but pause when I see four EMTs, transporting my grandma on a stretcher. I jog back down those several steps, to make room for them. I rush to the side of the stretcher, and catch a glimpse of my grandma. I call out her name but she doesn't respond.

"Sir, I'm going to have to ask you to step back." One of EMTs say.

"That's my grandma. What's going on?" I ask matching their pace, as they make their way to the ambulance.

"Sir." A female's voice interrupts me. I turn around and find one of the EMTs beside me. "A 9-1-1 call was made from inside of this house. Your grandma was complaining about chest pains and not being able to breathe. When we got here, we found her unconscious, not breathing well, and unresponsive. I noticed her medical alert bracelet which alerts us that she doesn't want to be resuscitated at any time."

"She didn't know what the hell she was thinking when she made that choice. You do whatever it takes to bring her back." I yell in anger.

"Sir I'm sorry and I know this is a tough time for you,

but we have to honor our patient's wishes. With that being said, she'll have to come to on her own. Right now we're giving your grandma oxygen."

My mind goes blank and my body becomes numb. Everything that the EMT was saying, was going in one ear and out the other. My body was officially operating on autopilot.

"Sir, you can ride in the back with your grandma."

I nod my head acknowledging that I heard her and I unconsciously move until I'm sitting in the back of the ambulance with my ma.

sixteen
Nyla

I was out visiting with a couple of old friends that I knew still lived in the area, when I got a call from Caleb letting me know that Mason's grandma was in the hospital.

I speed down the freeway, making my way to East Sacramento Hospital. As soon as I find parking, I rush through the automatic doors, bypassing the elevators, and making my way down a long hallway until I reach the doors that lead to the stairwell. Going by instructions alone provided by Caleb, I run up several flights of stairs, until I make it to the fourth floor to where the ICU unit was located.

I looked around the waiting room and find Brooke, Mason, Caleb, and the rest of the band sitting there. I stand there glued to my spot for several minutes unnoticed, until Caleb lifts his head and sees me standing there. He stands and walks in my direction. I look around him and I see Mason, but he wasn't paying anyone attention. My eyes leave him and connect with Brooke's. She gives me a sad smile, then wipes a tear from her eye.

"It's not good Nyla. She was found unconscious and not breathing well." Caleb explains.

"Has there been any changes in her condition?"

"No. She wears one of those medical alert bracelets letting them know to not resuscitate her. She's going to have to wake up on her own. Only thing they're giving her is oxygen to help with the breathing that she's still struggling with.

"I have to see him."

"Nyla, give him some time. He's been sitting there like a zombie for the past hour or so. We've all tried talking to him, but he won't respond."

I look over at Mason again, but my attention is averted to a doctor heading in his direction. Brooke blocks the doctor's path, and he stops. From what I could see from where I was standing, he was giving her an update on her grandma. He walks away and Brooke walks over to Mason, kneels down and starts talking to him. When she's done, he nods his head yes and she turns around and walks down the hall, and disappears into one of the rooms.

Ten minutes later I find myself pacing back and forth, unable to be still. I wanted to go over and comfort Mason, but I decided to keep my distance. *Did he know I was there for him?* I continue to pace, when a noise rings out on the floor.

"Code blue!" A nurse shouts from behind the counter.

Several doctors and nurses scramble from out of nowhere and they make their way down the hall, in the same direction Brooke went.

Mason immediately comes to a standing position and starts making his way towards his grandma's room.

I follow behind him, keeping a safe distance, but stop when I see all the doctors and nurses walk out the room. The doctor that was assigned to his ma, walks over to Mason and delivers the devastating news.

Mason falls to his knees and the most pain filled noise escapes his mouth.

I stand in the middle of the hall feeling every bit of his pain. My tears start to cloud my eyes. I blink and allow them to run down my face, to a point I was unable to stop them from flowing.

seventeen
Mason

It felt like I was on that floor forever, but I find the strength and come to my feet. I walk over to the closed door of my ma's room. I look through the small window and see my sister's body sprawled over her, screaming and crying.

I rest my head against the door and I continue to let my tears run down my face. I take a deep breath and I push the door open. Brooke looks up from my grandma, with mascara streaking down her face. I walk around the hospital bed that held my grandma's lifeless body, and when I'm close enough, Brooke gets off the bed and into my arms.

"She's g-gone." She weeps into my chest.

I embrace her. Holding her as tight as I possibly could.

"It's okay. It's going to be alright. She can finally rest now." I say in a tear filled, strained voice.

We stand there holding each other for god knows how long with just the sounds of our sobs echoing throughout the room.

The sound of footsteps catches my attention. I look towards the door and see a nurse walk in, and Nyla standing in the door frame with red eyes filled with unshed tears. I move my attention back to the nurse and see her removing tubes and cutting off machines around her.

"Mason." I hear Nyla whisper my name. I turn my head and find her standing in front of me. "I'm so sorry." She says covering her mouth with her hands.

I look at her with tears clouding my vision, unable to respond. Even though I knew this day was coming, I was still in shock.

"I'm heading home. If you need me. Please call me okay?" She says with a look of sadness in her eyes. With one final look at my grandma, then at Brooke and I. She gives me a slight wave of a goodbye, then she turns around and leaves.

* * *

The last couple of days went by in a blur. Three days ago, my ma passed and today we were saying our final farewell to a woman that did whatever she needed to make sure that my sister and I was taken care of. Unlike my bitch of a mother.

My phone rang nonstop, people were stopping by my ma's place I guess to give my sister and I their sympathy, but we really didn't know because we avoided everyone.

I found myself not being able sleep. The only way I could was with the assistance of a bottle of tequila or whatever liquor I could get my hands on. What I really wanted and craved was Nyla. I wanted her. All I needed was to feel her touch, and I knew I would be okay. I ignored every call, text, and I'm sure visit from her. I know she knows I'm grieving and I hope she understood it had nothing to do with her. It was just my fucked up way with handling my emotions. Most people wanted to have their friends and family around. Not me. Brooke seemed to be handling the death of our grandmother better than me. Yesterday she told me that she was going to stay with a friend on campus. I guess my behavior was depressing her.

I'm standing in my bathroom looking in the mirror at my pale complexion. My face was slimmer than I remembered. I had a beard now, dark puffy circles under my eyes, and I smelled. I pause my examination of myself when I hear the creaking of the front door opening and closing.

I walk down the hall making my way to the front of the house.

"Hey Brooke. Have you seen my suit?" I ask out loud. "I've looked everywhere for it and can't seem to find it."

I walk into the living room, and stop dead in my tracks.

"It's just me." Nyla responds. "Brooke gave me the key to the house. She's running a little late, so she asked me to pick up your suit from the cleaners and bring it to you. She'll be here shortly." She says sounding congested, then she sneezes. She grabs a tissue from the tissue box sitting on the coffee table and wipes her nose.

"Bless you."

She looks up at me shocked that I was speaking to her, since I've been avoiding her for the past couple of days. She stuffs the tissue into the pockets of her black two-piece suit jacket, and walks over to me. Looking me up and down.

"Come on. Let's get you ready."

She grabs my hand and pulls me down the hall until she finds the bathroom pulling me inside. She releases my hand and opens the small linen closet in the bathroom, and pulls out a washcloth and towel for me. She turns around and pulls the shower curtain back and starts the shower.

"I'll leave you, so you can shower. I'll be waiting in the

hallway. When you're done, I'll help you shave."

She walks around me and leaves shutting the door behind her.

I strip out of my clothes, then I shower and wash my hair. Totally forgetting the way water felt against my skin. *Had it been that long?* The sound of the shower cutting off let's Nyla know that I'm done. As soon as I wrap the towel around my waist, she opens the door and steps inside.

"Now you need a shave."

She opens the medicine cabinet and pulls out a fresh razor and shaving cream. I'm standing in front of her, watching her every move. She cuts on the water, and puts a small amount of shaving cream on her hand, then gently applies it to my face.

She picks up the razor and shaves me in complete silence. From time to time I would catch her biting her lip in concentration, or her eyes would briefly lock with mine.

"All done."

Nyla cuts the water off and wipes the remaining shaving cream from my face.

"I'm sure Brooke and the guys are on their way over. Don't forget your suit is up front on the couch. I'm going to head back to the house to start some of my packing before the service." She says avoiding eye contact with me.

"Wait. What?" I speak louder than I should. Startling her a bit. "You're leaving?"

"Yes I leave for New York tomorrow afternoon." She pauses. She stands there for a moment with a look of confusion on her face. "Mason when was the last time you spoke with Caleb or any of the other band members?"

"I haven't." I respond with regret.

"Well I'm going to let them tell you the news, but yes I leave tomorrow..." She stops and starts coughing, then sneezes several times.

I grab several tissues and I hand them to her.

"Thank you." She says while grabbing the tissues from my hand.

She pushes a strand of her now straight hair behind her ear, then she starts rocking back and forth, trying to debate on what to do next. Was she trying to find a way to leave? I wouldn't blame her since I've ignored her these past couple of days.

"Look Mason. I have to go. I've got to run by the pharmacy and pick up my antibiotics. I went to the doctor this morning and found out I have a sinus infection. I guess it's due to the climate change, and it doesn't help that I already suffer from allergies." She rambles off. "I'll see you later okay?"

She turns around and starts to leave, before she could go any further my hand reaches out and grabs hers. She stops but doesn't turn around to look at me.

"Thank you Nyla. For everything." I squeeze her hand before releasing it.

"Any time." She responds. She walks down the hallway with me standing in the doorway of the bathroom watching her. My eyes stay glued on her form until she turns the corner and disappears from my line of sight. I hear the front door close, signaling to me that she was gone.

* * *

"Dearly beloved. We gather here...." The minister continues.

The weather was cooler than normal on this spring day as we stood outside in the grave yard, paying our final respects to my ma. Brooke and I didn't want nothing too big. Something intimate, so it was just the two of us, a couple of her friends that knew our grandma, the band, and of course Nyla.

My dry eyes were on the white casket, that's covered in white and red roses, ma's favorite. I turn my head and see Nyla standing between Jax and Caleb. Just like everyone else she was wearing a pair of sunglasses to shield her sad eyes. From time to time I would catch her lifting her glasses to wipe away her tears. Not one time did she ever look in my direction. I had a lot on my mind and so much to think about after Nyla left this morning. I realized too late that my ma wouldn't want me in this state of mind, and pushing away the people I cared about the most. I knew it wasn't going to happen overnight, but I had to get my shit together, and move on because life was too short. Right? Brooke needed me and it was time for us to move onto the next stage of our lives.

This afternoon when Brooke came back home, bringing Jax, Evan, Jeremy, and Caleb with her. Caleb told me that we were flying out to Los Angeles Monday. He mentioned something about a possible recording deal with Rocktown Records, and that his dad wouldn't go into much detail, but he wanted to see us no later than Tuesday. Then we would fly out from Los Angeles to Toronto Friday. Since we already had our plane tickets scheduled to leave out to Los Angeles, we were able to swap them out for earlier flights. From our understanding we wouldn't be coming back to Sacramento, until after the tour. So we had a lot to do before we left.

With Brooke being in college, she decided she would stay here, then if everything went well with Rocktown Records, she would fly out to her city of choice to watch us perform in concert. She stood beside me, holding onto my arm. I pull my gaze away from Nyla and I look down at sister. She gives me a small smile and we turn our attention back to the minister.

Everything was going to be alright.

*   *   *

"Should we keep these?" Brooke asks me.

I turn around and see her holding a box full of stuff. I take them from her hands and put them on my bed. I rummage through them, not seeing anything too important, but several photo albums that we could keep. "Here, put these away for safe keeping." I say passing the albums to her.

"Okay."

I turn around and finish removing clothes from my old closet, and into a box marked charity.

"I've been staying at Caleb's house." Brooke says out of the blue.

I turn around and I look at her.

"What are you talking about?"

"I couldn't stand looking at you let your life wither away, so I stayed over there. Nyla was nice enough to let me stay in her room."

"Where did she stay?" I asked shocked by her confession. All this time I thought she was staying with a friend on campus. "How has she been?"

"Didn't you talk to her when she was here?"

"Not really."

Shaking her head, she continues. "She's been okay I guess. We talked. She always asks how you're doing. You need to talk to her."

"I will."

"When?"

"I will."

"Fine. Are you staying here tonight or are you going home?"

"I haven't decided yet."

"Well I'm staying there another night, so I can gather my stuff and bring it back here. I guess you'll be sleeping on the couch if you do decide to go home, because Nyla's been using your room." She says staring at me, waiting on my reaction. "Well I guess I'll leave you to your cleaning then. Later bro." She says before walking out my room.

"Later."

eighteen
Nyla

The soft strumming sounds of a guitar, has me opening my eyes and sitting up in bed. I turn towards the sound and I find Mason sitting back in his oversized chair with one of his guitars in his hands, deep in thought.

"Caleb told me that your flight is leaving out Sunday night instead of in the afternoon." He says turning his attention to me.

I pull the covers away from my body, not responding to his statement. I crawl to the side of the bed towards him, and I sit there looking at him. He places the guitar back on its stand, and he runs his hands down his face and looks at me.

"I see you decided to come back home. Give me a minute and I'll be out your way." I say, coming to my feet.

"Nyla stay. I don't want you to go."

I sit back down not saying a word.

"I'm sorry for how I've been treating you for the past

172

couple of days. I did receive all your texts and I ignored all your calls because I didn't want you to see me vulnerable and in a broken state."

"Mason."

"Nyla please let me finish. You have been nothing but a breath of fresh air for me. Brooke and ma were all I have. My mom is in jail and I have no clue to who my father is. When my grandma was first diagnosed with cancer, I shut myself out until she knocked some sense into me, by telling me that she was going to fight as long as she could, but I needed to be strong with her. That there was no room to be depressed when depression just makes you sick, and she didn't need my emotional state bringing her down. So when I was around her I stayed positive. On my bad days you could find me at The Grind tossing back drinks trying to numb my pain. I've even tried various drugs, but after that day when my grandma found me in bed with those two girls. I knew I needed help, so I checked myself into rehab for about a month. How selfish of me right? It only caused my grandma more pain."

"Mason you have to stop being so hard on yourself. You couldn't have prevented what happened to your grandma."

He keeps his eyes on me and continues.

"Then you came along." He pauses. "You're beautiful, smart, positive, and caring. You come from a wonderful family with both a mom and dad I'm sure love you so very much. Unfortunately, I didn't have that but my grandma was one helluva woman who played both roles and did all she could to make sure Brooke and I had a good childhood."

My heart was breaking listening to his story. I wipe away the tear falling down my cheek and I sit there giving him all my support. Showing him that I was there for him and I felt his pain.

"I didn't mean to make you cry with my sob story. I just wanted you to know that my distance had nothing to do with you. If anything I want you in my life. I'm not perfect Nyla, but I would like to see where this could go."

"You say that now. You just wait until you have millions of girls screaming out your name, I'm sure you'll forget about me."

"Nyla don't say that. I could never forget you. It's only two weeks." He says running a frustrated hand through his hair. "Before you know it I'll be back here in California, making plans to come and visit you in New York."

"You make it sound so easy. Don't you know that those

two weeks can turn into possible months. I'm sure Caleb told you about you guys signing a possible recording deal, so you don't know what's going to happen."

After that last statement, we sit there in complete silence, realizing that our time together was being cut short and coming to an end very soon.

"How about we take it one day at a time." I break the silence.

"One day at a time huh?" He asks me.

"Yes. Let's not make any promises. Whatever happens. Happens."

"Okay I can do that."

"Come here." I scoot back to make room for him.

He stands and removes his shirt, jeans and shoes, and gets in beside me and pulls me into his arms. I snuggle up against him, laying my head on his chest and I close my eyes. He wraps his arm around me and kisses the top of my head.

"I'm so exhausted. I haven't slept in days."

"I know. I haven't slept much either because I was too busy

worrying about you."

His hand runs underneath the t-shirt that I was wearing. I could feel his warm touch against my back, trailing up and down my spine in a soothing motion. Until his movements stop. Lifting my head, I look down and see his eyes closed. I sit up and straddle his hips, then I lean forward and place a kiss against his lips. His eyes flutter open, and I lower my head and kiss him again.

"Nyla." He moans out my name.

"Shhh. Try and get some sleep."

I trail my kisses down to his neck, chest, all the way down his hard abs until I reach the waist band of his boxers. I reach inside and come in contact with his dick. I withdraw my hand, releasing him from his boxers.

"Nyla." He moans my name again.

Gripping him in my hand, I begin a slow stroke up and down his length.

"I'm going to help you sleep better." Are the words that I speak before my head lowers and his hard flesh slides between my lips.

176

"Aaaaaah." Mason yells out, gripping the sheet between his hands. "Mmm fuck."

My mouth continues to suck, while my tongue swirls and tastes every inch of him.

I look up from my position and see Mason looking down at me with hooded eyes. Just the look of exhaustion and pleasure on his face, just encourages me even more to pleasure him. I close my eyes and I continue to move my head up and down.

Mason reaches down and runs a hand through my hair, and along my scalp. Gently placing his hand behind my head he urges me to go a little faster.

"Nyla I'm about to come."

But I don't stop.

"Nyla baby. Did you hear me?"

I did, but I continue tasting him.

"Nyla." He shouts my name, before he fills my mouth, draining himself of his desire. When I knew he had nothing left, I kiss my way back up his body, and I lay against his body, with my chest against his. Where I can feel his rapid heartbeat.

"Nyla." He says my name, sounding exhausted and drained.

I place my lips against his ear and I whisper to him to get some sleep. He wraps his arms around my body and we lay there in complete silence until sleep finally takes over.

nineteen
Mason

"Nyla. Wake up."

Rubbing my hand down her back, I continue down until it rests upon her ass. Giving it a little squeeze. She stirs awake and lifts her head off my chest.

"Good morning."

"Good morning." She responds, coming to a sitting position on top of me. "How did you sleep?"

"Great." I respond, then I come to a sitting position. Wrapping my arms around her, I lean forward and place several kisses along her collar bone. "Your flight is scheduled to leave in five hours."

"Did we sleep that late?"

"I guess we really needed to catch up on our sleep."

"I guess so." She says giving me a sad smile.

We sit there staring at each other. With silence filling the air.

"I hate that you have to leave so early."

"Mason."

"I'm going to miss you like crazy." I confess. "Are you going to miss me?" I ask while looking into her eyes

She averts eye contact. Trying to avoid this conversation. She shifts in my arms trying to remove herself from my lap. I tighten my arms around her waist keeping her in place.

"Answer me Nyla."

"Yes." She says looking me in my eyes.

"Then stay."

"What?"

"You can come out to Los Angeles with us. I'm sure Caleb's family would love to see you. Then you can return to New York from there."

She leans forward and kisses me. "Can I think about

it?"

I move bringing Nyla to her back, and I rest my hips between her legs.

"Well you better get to thinking." I lean down to kiss her lips. "Because in the meantime, I'm not letting you leave this bed."

twenty
Nyla

"Hello?" I answered my phone, not looking at the caller ID.

"Hello? Is that all you have to say to me? Girl I have been worried sick about you. You've been gone a little over a week and you have yet picked up your phone to let me know that you arrived in California safe!" Jordyn shouts through the phone.

"Jordyn I'm so sorry. I..."

"Don't Jordyn me and you can forget about apologizing. Next time remember to call or text. Something!"

"Okay. Okay! I'm sorry!" I respond genuinely.

"Fine! I forgive you. So how's your trip been going?"

"Crazy. I'm actually flying out tomorrow to Los Angeles, and I hope to be back in New York before the end of the week. So you'll be seeing me soon."

"Why?"

"Have you ever heard of Rocktown Records?"

"Girl you know I don't listen to rock."

"Well they want to give Wildfire a recording deal. They are really well known in the rock industry. I heard they've thought about expanding their clientele by signing other groups and solo artist that sing in different genres too. But anyway, Wildfire is leaving for Toronto soon, so if everything goes well, as I know it will. Wildfire is going to be huge."

"Are you fuckin' serious!" Jordyn screams on the other end, causing me to pull away from the phone.

"Girl do you realize that your best friend is going to be a fuckin' rock star! Bitch you better make sure you get me an autograph before you leave."

"You've never even heard them play."

"Don't have to. I'll just go by what you've told me. Do you think we could get tickets to one of their shows?"

"How did this conversation go from you going off on me for not calling, to wanting to go to a rock concert?" I say laughing. "Look I'll have to talk to you later. Mason and I are going out, so I have to finish getting ready."

"Who's Mason?"

"Bye Jordyn."

I disconnect the call and continue getting ready. Forty minutes later I stand in front of the mirror looking at myself, making sure nothing was out of place. My hair was blown out and flat ironed straight. I was wearing a form fitting simple light gray lace sundress that reminded me of Mason's eyes, and my makeup consisted of mascara, a little foundation, and my favorite nude gloss. I slip on a pair of black wedges and I grab my small black and gray clutch off the dresser before heading out my bedroom door.

Walking down the hall, I hear the guys laughing and talking in the living room. They were talking about how excited they were about their upcoming trip to Los Angeles and Toronto. When I step into the living room, all conversation ceases.

"Damn girl!" Yelled Jax, Jeremy, and Evan in unison.

Mason stands from his seat and walks towards me with a look of appreciation on his face. He was wearing a pair of dark washed out jeans, and a white button down dress shirt rolled to quarter sleeves, with a pair of all white

Converse sneakers.

"You look amazing." He says grabbing my hand.

"Thank you. You look really nice yourself."

"Thanks. Are you ready?"

"Definitely."

He kisses the top of my hand and turns around and walks me to the door.

"Bye you guys." I wave in their directions.

"Bye Nyla." They say in unison again.

"Hey Mason. Make sure you have her home at decent time." Caleb jokes, coming out of the kitchen with a bowl of chips. "Nyla you know where to find me if he fucks up."

Raising his right hand in the air, Mason flips them all off before we walk out the door.

Walking down the sidewalk I notice an all-black SUV pulled in front of the driveway, with I assumed was the driver standing beside the back door.

"Eddie." Mason calls the driver by name when we approach.

"Mason." He responds before opening the door for us. I step inside with the assistance from Mason and he climbs in after me.

"You hired a driver?"

"No. Caleb told me that his dad uses him from time to time, and he suggested I call him."

"Okay." I respond while watching the driver get into the car.

"Nyla." Mason whispers in my ear.

His lips touch the side of my neck and a shiver goes down the spine of my back.

"You look really sexy tonight." He says pulling away from my neck.

"I know." I laugh. "So where are you taking me?" I ask turning in my seat to face him.

"You'll find out soon enough." He responds, giving me

no more details.

Turning around in my seat I look out the window at our surroundings, trying to figure out where we're going. Nothing was coming to mind at the moment.

After forty-five minutes of light conversation and me grilling Mason for clues of where we were going, I finally figured it out.

"Are we going to Caleb's families' vacation house?"

"Yes." He smiles at me. "I hope you don't mind, but I kind of wanted you all to myself tonight with no interruptions. So when I told Caleb what my plans were, he handed over the keys to the house with no hesitation."

"I don't mind at all. I use to love coming here when I was a kid during the summer. I can't believe his family still owns this property."

"Yeah when his dad wants to get away, he still brings Mrs. Walker out here for peace and quiet."

Ten minutes later, the SUV comes to a stop and the driver hops out and opens my door. Grabbing his outreached hand, he helps me out. I walk up the driveway and stop to look at the lake cabin in front of me.

After a couple of minutes of conversation with Eddie, Mason catches up to me and leads me up the walk way to the house. With his hand at the small of my back he unlocks the door and leads me inside.

He cuts the light switch on and the room illuminates. I look around the familiar space that currently housed updated furnishings.

"I was thinking we could roast hotdogs and s'mores over the fire pit on the deck. Can you grab some blankets, and if you want you can head outside. I'm going to grab all the supplies I need and I will meet you out there."

"Okay."

I walk down the hall to the linen closet and I pull out two throw blankets, then I walk back down the hall stopping in the open doorway of the bedroom that Caleb and I use to share when we would visit during the summer. A king size bed now sat in the middle of the room, replacing the bunk beds that he and I would sleep in. Stepping away from the doorway, I continue down the hall, stopping briefly in the open family room leading into the kitchen.

"Do you need any help?"

"I think I got it." Mason winks at me and turns back to his task at hand.

"I'll be outside if you need me." I call over my shoulder.

I open the back door leading out to the deck, and I walk outside and along the stone pathway, lit up by outdoor solar lights. I Continue along the short path listening to the sounds of crickets and from time to time I would catch a glimpse of a firefly. Just the sight of them reminded of the times when me, Caleb and my dad; when my family was able to come along, would make it a contest to see who could catch the most fireflies in a jar, and by the end of the night, we would release them.

I walk up the two steps of the deck and I toss the throw blankets on the large outdoor chaise lounge chair. I walk around the already lit fire pit and I stand resting my arms against the rail of the deck looking down at the view before me of the city of Sacramento.

The sky was black with just a couple of specks of stars in it, and the rest of the area surrounding us was covered in various plants and trees. Standing here I now remembered why I loved being out here. It was calming.

The sound of footsteps has me turning my gaze from

the view, to Mason, who was carrying a large basket and one of Caleb's many acoustic guitars. He places the basket beside the fire pit, and sits the guitar against the chaise lounge chair. Showing me his sexy grin, he walks over to me and places his hands on either side of me, caging me in. I lean back against the rail, so I could look up at him.

"Are you hungry?" He asks staring down at my lips.

"Very." I respond with a smile on my lips.

He lowers his head and kisses my forehead and grabs my hand and we walk over to the chaise lounge where we roast our hotdogs over the pit, while laughing and talking about all the mischief I use to get into out here.

"I remember the time when Caleb and I were out front playing tag. I was running away from him and not paying attention to where I was going, and ran into a tree."

Mason starts laughing his ass off.

"It's not funny. My eye swelled up so big that night. I'm glad the next morning when I woke up, the swelling was gone and only a scratch was left behind. Now that I think of it, I didn't see that tree in the front." I pause. "That's right!" I snap my fingers. "Caleb's dad had someone to come out and cut it down. I guess he felt sorry for me since I hit that tree pretty damn hard."

"Damn Nyla." He says calming his laugh.

"So what time is Eddie coming back to get us?"

"I told him that I would call him. Why? Are you in a hurry to get back?"

I pause and I look at him. If he only knew how bad I would love spending all my time here with him. So instead of responding, I lean forward and I kiss his lips, sliding my tongue between his slightly parted lips to get a brief taste of him, eliciting a low moan from him. I pull my lips away and I stand and gather all of our plates.

"I'm going to take these back to the house." I say avoiding eye contact with him.

I quickly turn away and jog down the steps of the deck and hurry back to the house.

Rushing through the back door of the house, I walk inside, forgetting to close the door behind me. I walk into the kitchen and place the plates into the sink. I turn the faucet on and I stand there watching the water run over the plates, while in a daze trying to get my emotions back in order.

I continue to watch the water as it starts to fill the sink up. I didn't even hear the back door shut or realized I was no longer alone in the house, until a pair of strong arms wrap around my waist. Mason reaches out and cuts the water off before turning me around to face him. Looking down at me he begins searching my eyes with a look of concern on his gorgeous face.

"Come on." He says pulling me away from the sink by my hand.

We walk into the family room, and that's when I realize soft music was playing.

He stops and turns around and pulls me close to his body, and wraps his arms securely around my waist, and I follow by sliding my hands up his chest, to rest my arms around his neck.

We move to the music, while getting lost into each other's senses of sound, touch, and eventually taste.

Grabbing me by the back of my head, he lowers his head and his lips tenderly touch mine. He slowly sucks on my top lip and does the same to my lower lip before sliding his tongue into my mouth.

My body starts to relax against his as he continues to make love to my mouth. At this point all I wanted was to feel his bare skin against mine, while having all his weight pressed on top of me. Needing to feel him inside me, marking me as his and only his.

Reaching between our bodies, I begin unbuttoning his shirt without breaking our kiss, going by feeling alone. When I reach the last button, I slide my hands up his hard abs, chest, reaching his shoulders, to push his shirt down his lean muscle arms and off.

Placing my hands on his belt, I unbuckle it and I tug until it's hanging loosely, then I release the button of his jeans, and I slowly slide his zipper all the way down, causing his jeans to hang low on his hips. I run my fingers tips along his boxers. My fingers were on a mission. Before they could go any further, Mason stops kissing me and grabs a hold of my wrists, stopping my movement. Stepping away from me, he releases my wrists and interlock his hands with mine and leads me further into the family room, stopping in front of the couch. Removing his shoes with his feet, he kicks them aside and places my hands back on his hips before kissing me again.

Taking that as my cue I slide his jeans off his hips until they drop around his ankles and his boxers soon follow. Stepping out of his clothes, he sits down on the coach and pulls my body forward. Sliding his hands up my legs, he reaches under my dress and pulls my panties down, while I pull my dress up my body and over my head until I'm standing in front of him naked.

Grabbing me by my ass, he pulls me closer and leans forwards and gently nips at my left nipple, then he does the same to the my right one, but tugging a little harder before releasing it with his teeth, then sucking the sting away with his lips.

Brushing his lips against my stomach. He places a trail of kisses where ever his lips touched. He leans back on the couch, bringing my body with him.

Placing my knees one by one on the couch I straddle his hips, feeling his warm and hard evidence between my legs, resting at my entrance.

"We'll make this work." He whispers against my neck.

He lowers his head placing kisses against my collarbone. Causing a whimper to escape from my lips.

I arch into him, when I feel his fingers digging into my hips.

Kissing his way up my neck and chin, he tugs my lower

lip between his teeth and releases it. With his eyes locked to mine, he tightens his grip on my hips, and he slowly guides me down his length, allowing me to feel every hard bare inch of him push inside me.

I bite down hard on my lower lip, moaning to myself, trying to prevent myself from screaming out loud.

"Baby I want to hear you. Don't hold it in. It's just you and me." He moans in response.

He felt so good, that I needed more of him. Rotating my hips, I slide further down his length, until he fills me completely.

"Mason." I scream out loud.

"I know Nyla." He responds in a tortured tone. I'm here." He says just before slipping two fingers into my mouth.

I continue to grind up and down his length, picking up my speed, moaning and sucking his fingers further into my mouth.

"Slow down." Mason says squeezing my hip with his free hand.

I nod my head in acknowledgment, and I slow down.

He withdraws his fingers from my mouth, and trails them over my lips.

Overcome with emotion, tears fill my eyes and begin falling down my cheeks.

He wipes away my tears with his thumbs, and brings my face down to his and kisses me deeply.

Scooting us to the edge of the coach, he drops to his knees and lowers us to the carpet without breaking our connection or kiss.

As soon as my back touches the carpet. Mason slides his arms underneath my back moving them up until, his hands reach the nape of my neck, sliding his fingers through my hair. He gently tugs at my roots, tilting my chin up, giving him better access to my neck.

He begins sucking and kissing along the side of my neck, while moving inside of me in a slow tortuous motion.

Before my scream could slip from my lips, his mouth covers mine in a sweet demanding kiss.

Slowly he pulls his lips away until they're less than an

inch apart from mine. He looks down at with me and I can see the emotion displayed in his eyes. *Was it love, lust, confusion, or regret?*

"Nyla I'm not wearing a condom."

"Birth control." I respond in a breathless moan.

His hips rotate and thrust forward, causing him to sink deeper.

"Fuck!" I shout out in both pain and pleasure, from what I felt from the sting of the carpet burn against my back, and what he was doing between my legs.

"Do I have permission to come inside you Nyla?" He whispers in my ear, and sucks my earlobe between his lips.

I run my nails against his back, and I continue down until I'm grasping his ass.

"You'll be the first." I whisper in response, feeling drained and spent.

He lowers his head until our nose touch. "Please promise me that we'll try to make this work."

"I promise." I say before turning my head away, I bite

down on his shoulder, coming hard against him.

"You're so beautiful when you come. Why did you turn your head away from me?" He asks while thrusting harder inside me. "Nyla." He moans my name out into the side of my neck, letting go of his release inside of me.

He lifts his head away from my neck, and places a kiss to my chin.

"We'll make this work." He says, before kissing me long and hard.

twenty-one
Caleb

After a long flight of having Jax snoring in my ear, a child who wouldn't stop kicking my chair, and suffering from starvation because the flight attendants didn't believe in passing out extra snacks because it was against their policy. I was happy to finally pull up in front of my parent's house.

"Dude your parent's house is huge!" Jeremy says when our taxi comes to a stop. We all exit, and start stretching our limbs.

The driver unloads the van, I tip him, and send him on his way. Then we all walk up the path leading to my parent's house.

"How long have your parent's lived in this house?" Jax asks.

"They moved in two years ago."

"I want a house like this." Evan responds.

"Maybe if you stop spending your money on women,

maybe you could." Mason says, laughing to himself.

"So are you a one-woman fuckin' man now or something?"

"Something like that." Mason responds while looking in Nyla's direction.

"We'll see how long that will last." Evan laughs out.

"Would all of you shut the fuck up please! I'm tired, hungry, and I could use a shower!" I shout.

We walk up the few steps in silence to the front door. Before we could take another step, the door swings open.

"I was starting to think you weren't going to show." My mom says with a huge smile on her face.

She stood in the doorway in a light blue sundress, with her hair pulled away from her face in a ponytail. Her light green eyes moved from me then to Nyla and the fellas.

"Look at you guys!" She says placing her hands on each of our faces, looking us over before pulling each of us in a tight hug. "It's so good to see all of you." She says holding onto Mason.

"It's good to see you too Mrs. Walker." Mason responds, returning the embrace.

"I'm really sorry to hear about your grandma. How are you holding up?"

"I'm doing better. Thanks for asking."

"And Brooke?"

"She's keeping her head in her books."

They pull away and she turns her attention to Nyla.

With a bigger smile on her face she pulls Nyla into a tight hug. "How have you been? Gosh look how beautiful you are!" How are your parents?"

"They're good. Dad's enjoying retirement and mom volunteers at the hospital from time to time when they're not traveling. The last time I talked to them they were enjoying the beautiful villages of Italy."

"I'm sure they're loving it! I remember when Isaac took us there on our wedding anniversary. It's really a beautiful place. Matter of fact I have a photo album full of pictures I'll show you when we get inside."

My mom grabs Nyla's hand and everyone walks up the remaining stairs to the house, leaving me behind.

"Are you coming?" Nyla asks.

Clearing my thoughts, I look around and see everyone looking at me.

"Yeah give me a minute."

"Alright son." My mom responds, winking in my direction.

They continue their walk up the stairs until they reach the door. My mom pushes the door open and they all walk in.

I look around the property taking in the view. I could count on one hand on how many times I'd been out here. My dad had it built for my mom exactly how she wanted it. I guess he felt obligated after all the rumors and scandals about him being seen with various women when they first signed their big record deal several years ago, and he was able to hide it from my mom. A lot happened around that time that caused my parents to separate for a while. All this happened around the time Nyla moved to California. Until this day, Nyla thinks my dad was always on tour with his band, but she never knew the real reason why. She just knew that he was gone a lot, and when he was home, we acted like what society claimed to be a normal happy family.

I knew my mom forgave him for all his cheating, but the reason for their separation was still unknown to me. Now I had to go in here and act like we were one happy family.

I jog up the stairs and walk through the door and see Nyla hugging my dad. When his gray eyes land on me, he kisses her on the cheek and walks in my direction.

"Son."

"Dad."

"Have a good trip?"

"Yeah." I lied.

"Good to hear." He says before turning his attention away from me. "Well boys while Mrs. Walker and Nyla finish up dinner, we'll head to the studio to discuss business." He announces.

We walk through the kitchen and down a small hall leading to my dad's studio slash office. We walk through the door and I see Richie, my dad's lawyer and manager sitting in a chair in front of the desk, looking through some paperwork. When he sees us, he puts it away and stands.

"Caleb." He says extending his hand.

"Rich." I respond and I shake his hand.

My dad was currently sitting behind his desk, and the rest of the band and I continue to stand. Currently my mind was trying to process why Rich was even here.

"Not trying to be rude, but why is he here?" I ask directing my attention to my dad.

"I can answer that." Rich responds. "I invited myself actually because I had more paperwork I had to draw up, that we all have to go over before you guys leave on Wednesday."

"Wednesday? That's the day after tomorrow! I thought we were leaving Friday?"

"We were until we got a call about two hours ago from Rocktown Records." Rich responds.

"What is he talking about?" I ask my dad.

"Rocktown records wants to sign Wildfire immediately. It just so happens; they were in town the other night when you guys were performing your last show at The Grind. They were very impressed. Caleb when they found out that you were Isaac Walker's son along with that, they immediately wanted to sign you guys." Rich speaks up.

"Are you serious? I thought they wanted to see us perform on tour with Hurricane first before they made their decision." I respond.

"Yes Caleb. Very serious. Congratulations! Your hard work has finally paid off."

Jax, Mason, Evan, and Jeremy had looks on their faces like they couldn't believe everything was happening so fast.

"I'm not believing this." I say finally, taking a seat in the vacant seat beside Rich.

"Why the change in plans? It's kind of short notice."

"They want you guys in the studio as soon as possible to record a few songs. After the two-week tour ends with Hurricane, they want to schedule you guys for another tour to give you guys some more exposure and publicity. Before you know it you guys will be climbing the music charts. Can't help to say it, but that's the music business for you." My dad says kneeling beside me.

"Does mom know?"

"Yes. And she's very excited and happy for you."

"These contracts need to be signed by all of you by tomorrow afternoon." Rich says.

I remove them from his outstretched hand, and I look down at the papers, not believing that our band was actually getting signed, then we were scheduled for a two-week city tour, and possibly another one once our tour ended with Hurricane. What was I going to tell Nyla?

As if reading my mind, my dad answers my question.

"I know Nyla was supposed to be here for a couple of days, but unfortunately she's going to have to cut her trip short."

"Maybe she could go with us. Just for a couple of days. Rich do you think we could make that happen?"

"Sorry Caleb. But in this case the only females allowed on tour are the wives. I know she's like family to you but those are the rules. Now when you guys sign your own recording deal etc. Then we can talk." Rich responds.

"So there's no women allowed on the tour bus?" Evan asks.

"You guys are going to have a pretty busy schedule. You'll have females throwing themselves at you once they hear you guys play. I don't care about how many women you have in your hotel room, but none on the tour bus." My dad responds.

"Dad."

"Listen Caleb. I know what I'm talking about. You know your mom and I almost didn't make it."

"Yeah because you couldn't keep your dick in your pants."

The room falls silent after my confession.

"I know. That's why every time I go on tour she's by my side. The shit you're talking about happened years ago, and your mom has forgiven me. Why do you think I'm telling you all this? Guys if you really take your music seriously, being in a relationship with anyone right now, will not work. When you're on tour, everywhere you turn there will be females advertising free pussy."

"That's nothing new. They do it now." Jax responds.

"I'm not talking about local club groupies Jax. There are women out there who are pros at doing this. Either they're trying to earn a free ride to stardom by offering a few blow jobs, a quick fuck, or they are trying to ruin your career before it can even get started. Do you guys understand?"

"Yeah." We all say in unison.

"Good, now leave those papers on my desk and I want all of you to try and enjoy the rest of your night. Because after Wednesday, there's no telling when you'll have a break to do anything."

I lay the papers down on the desk, and I stand.

"Son make sure you tell Nyla about the change of plans with the tour, and I'll see if I can get her a plane ticket back to New York tomorrow morning."

With one final look in my dad and Rich's direction, we leave.

twenty-two
Nyla

"How's school going?"

I look up from the photo album from my spot at the table, and at Mrs. Walker, who was busy preparing a salad.

"Tough. I'm so close to getting my Bachelors in Biology. Once I'm done with that I start my other medical training and residency."

"That's so amazing. I'm so proud of you Nyla."

"Thank you. It's feels like I've been in school forever, then I think about how much school I have left."

"Well keep up the good work. Have you decided on what field you wanted to go into?"

"I'm leaning towards women's health. My aunt was an Obstetrician-Gynecologist, and I've decided to follow in her footsteps."

"That's wonderful." She says while dicing tomatoes.

I look back down at the photo album and I start turning the pages, coming across familiar images until I see a photo wedged between the pages. I pull it out, and I see a picture of a little boy that looked to be around the age of three years old, smiling bright with his eyes closed tight. After further inspection of the photo, I knew he was actually laughing. He was standing beside Mr. Walker, who was looking down at him with a smile on his face, and they were holding hands. I frown when I notice the little boy in the photo had dark hair instead of blond.

"Mrs. Walker. Who is this?"

She puts the knife she was using to chop up the vegetables down on the cutting board, and she comes around the counter to get a better look. When she sees the picture her face suddenly goes pale. With a shaky hand she reaches out and takes the photo from my hands.

"I'm not sure Nyla." She responds in a hurried manner, then shoves the photo in the pocket of her sundress. With nothing left to say she walks back around the counter and resumes her chopping.

What just happened?

The sound of voices coming down the hall, redirects my attention.

"Hey boys." Mrs. Walker says. She touches her face and wipes away a tear.

Is she crying?

"Why don't you all head upstairs and wash up for dinner. It should be ready in about forty-five minutes. Help yourselves to any room." She continues.

Evan, Jeremy, and Jax leave the kitchen and jog up the stairs.

I close the photo album and I place it on the counter.

"Here you go Mrs. Walker."

"Thank you Nyla. Just leave it right there and I'll get it later." She responds, not wanting to look up at me.

"Are you alright?" I ask her.

"Yes Nyla. I'm just fine. Do you mind finishing up the salad for me? I'm going to head up stairs for a minute."

"Sure." I respond, with concern in my voice.

"Thanks honey." She puts the knife down and rushes

out the kitchen.

I walk around the counter and resume making the salad.

"Hey." Mason whispers in my ear. Sneaking up behind me. He wraps his arms around my body pulls me against him.

"Hey." I respond turning around slowly in his arms.

I look over his shoulder to find Caleb standing behind him. Looking at us with a smile on his face. I Pull out of Mason's arms, and I turn my attention to Caleb.

"Hey you. Your mom let it slip about the official record deal." I say, giving him a sad smile. "I'm really happy for you guys."

"Thanks Nyla."

Reaching out, he grabs my hand and pulls me into a hug. "Too bad we haven't had much time to catch up."

"Well we still have a couple of days left."

"Actually we don't. We leave out Wednesday. Dad's in the process of getting you a plane ticket as we speak. So I guess you'll be leaving sooner than you thought."

"Wow! Well I guess I'll have to catch one of your concerts."

"Most definitely. I should have a schedule of our concert dates by tonight. I'll text you the info."

"Thanks."

"Yeah no problem. Where did my mom go?"

"Um she went upstairs for a minute."

"Well I'm going to head up and get some rest before dinner. Talk to you two later."

He walks off, leaving Mason and I standing there.

"Are you okay?" Mason asks me, with a look of concern on his face.

"Yes." I lied.

"Okay." He says staring down into my eyes. Not being able to help himself he tilts my head back and lowers his head to press his lips against mine. Sucking and tasting the gloss off my lips. He pulls his lips away, and we stand there resting our foreheads against each other, trying to calm our beating hearts.

I look up and see Mr. Walker looking at me and Mason. When he sees me looking in his direction, he leaves the kitchen.

Mason pulls me closer to his body and kisses my forehead. "Let's go upstairs."

"You go ahead. I'm going to stay here and finish up dinner until Mrs. Walker comes back down."

"Okay. I need to call Brooke and tell her the news."

"Okay." I respond.

He walks out of the kitchen and grabs our bags from the front foyer, before making his way upstairs.

I turn around and my eyes land on the photo album, with confusion clouding my thoughts.

* * *

After dinner, I finish up with the dishes and I make my way upstairs. I'm walking down the hall towards Mason's room when I hear the sound of Mr. and Mrs. Walker's voice. They were arguing and yelling at each other. Mrs. Walker never came back down for dinner, due to the fact she wasn't feeling well; which was the excuse Mr. Walker gave us when he showed up without her. I stop in front of their bedroom door, but all I could hear were low muffled voices now coming from the other side. Deciding to mind my own business I walk two doors down to Mason's room.

I open the door and I lock it behind me. The sound of the shower going and Mason's voice fills the room. I strip out of my clothes and I walk into the bathroom to see Mason's naked form through the fogged up glass door of the shower. I grab a wash cloth off the shelf near the sink then I pull the shower door open and I step in.

Mason stops singing and turns around and looks at me. He dips his head back under the shower head to wash away his shampoo. My eyes slowly roam over his slick hard body, then back up to a smiling face.

Man I was going to miss him.

"Hey." I step forward and I reach up to run my hands through his wet hair, bringing his head down so I could kiss him.

"What was that for?" He asks me, kissing my lips

again.

"Do I have to have a reason?"

"No. You can kiss me any time you want, and anywhere." He says with a sexy smile on his face.

I roll my eyes and shake my head to myself. I pour some body wash on my cloth and begin lathering my body.

"Caleb sent me a new tour schedule and it looks like you'll be in my area once the tour with Hurricane ends. I can't believe you guys are performing at the Madison Square Garden. Maybe Brooke can fly in around that time and she can stay with me if she wants. I don't have an extra room but she can take mine and I'll take the couch." I ramble on not noticing the silence coming from him. I stop talking and I look up at Mason to see if he was listening, and I see him in fact listening but not saying a word.

"Mason?"

"Do you realize that your plane leaves tomorrow morning and it will be awhile until I see you again?" He asks me.

"I know."

He grabs my right hand and places it over his heart, where I could feel his heart pounding hard in his chest.

"Do you feel that? This is what you do to me whenever you're around or when I'm just thinking about you." He says pulling my hand down from his chest to his stomach, then to finally rest between his legs. He manually wraps my fingers around his dick and directs my movements in an up and down motion. "I've never been in a long distance relationship, but I would try for you Nyla." He moans.

He pushes me gently against the tile wall and his mouth attacks mine. My arms wrap tightly around his neck and he lifts me up by the back of my thighs, and with one swift smooth motion, he enters me.

"Mmm." We moan in unison into each other's mouth.

He tears his mouth away and looks me in the eyes.

"I can't get enough of you." He whispers against my lips.

It's strange because I couldn't get enough of him either. It was as if he needed me and I needed him.

He made love to me against the shower wall until the

water started to turn cool, causing our bodies to shiver, and our fingertips showed signs of wrinkling.

* * *

The next morning Mason and I reluctantly pull our naked bodies away from each other. I showered alone this time, and did my daily morning routine.

After getting dressed I make my rounds around the house making sure to say goodbye to everyone.

Now Mason and I were outside waiting on my taxi to arrive.

"It's funny how my whole purpose for my trip was to spend it with Caleb, but somehow I was with you more." I say trying to lighten the mood.

"I can't help that I'm irresistible Nyla."

I turn to look at him standing beside me and I couldn't help but to laugh.

The sound of an incoming vehicle has us both turning our heads in its direction.

"That's me."

He pulls me close to his body and leans down and places his lips against mine, then he lifts his head. "I can ride to the airport with you."

"That's alright. I'm already having a hard time saying goodbye to you. I think it's best I go alone." I respond.

"Then I guess I'll see you soon. I promise to call and text you every chance I get."

"Promise?" I ask him.

He leans down and kisses my lips again, sealing his promise.

The taxi pulls up to the curb and stops. The driver gets out, gives his greetings and starts loading my things into the trunk. When he's done he gets back into the car.

"I have to go."

He pulls me into another hug.

"Bye Nyla." He whispers in my ear.

I turn my head until my nose touches his.

"See you later." I respond before touching my lips to his.

I pull away and I make my way to the taxi. I open the door and get in. The taxi pulls away from the curb and continues towards its destination. I sit there looking straight ahead and never looking back. The rest of my ride to the airport consisted of silence and tears.

twenty-three
Mason

Two Months Later. New York...

Caleb is it true that you're dating a super model?

Over here Jax. What designer are you wearing today?

Hey Mason are you single?

Were just some of the many questions being thrown at us as we make our way into one of New York's popular radio stations, 108.6 Rock On. It was official. We were now the hottest rock band signed to Rocktown Records. After our two-week tour with Hurricane. We hit the studio and recorded our first three singles that were now climbing the Rock Billboard Charts. Everywhere we turned we saw flashing lights from cameras, fans wanting our autographs, and our faces were plastered on every magazine.

The reporters continue to take our pictures and yell out their questions as we are led by our team of bodyguards past screaming fans holding up posters and screaming I love you. We finally make our way inside and hop on an elevator that would take us up to the eighteenth floor.

"Man, sometimes I feel like all of this is a dream." Evan speaks beside me. "Who would have thought just a month being signed to a label our single would be on top of the charts."

"I feel you on that man. I'm just excited to be in New York. Not everyone gets a chance to perform at Madison Square Garden." Jeremy says with a huge grin on his face. "So Mason why you so quiet man? Doesn't Nyla stay in this area?"

"Yeah she lives about fifteen minutes from our hotel."

"Well I know where you'll be crashing tonight." Caleb says from the other side of the elevator.

The elevator comes to a stop and we all exit.

"I know one thing. I hope you get some pussy soon because you've been walking around like you lost your damn best friend, when you could have had any girl you wanted. Matter of fact when we were in Detroit two nights ago, you had these women wanting you to partake in an orgy with you, and you turned them down. Were you losing your fuckin' mind?" Evan puts his two cents in.

"Man leave Mason alone. Maybe you should learn a

thing or two from him. At the rate you're going. You're going to end up catching a STD or your dick is going to fall off." Jax responds.

"You can't get a STD from a girl sucking on your dick." Evan says.

We all stop in the hallway and we all turn our attention to Evan.

"Can you?" He asks.

"Stupid ass." Caleb says under his breath.

We turn around and continue down the hall until we come to a desk with a middle aged receptionist sitting behind it. She's on the phone but when she sees us, she ends her call and stands up and starts squealing.

"Omigod. Wildfire my granddaughters and I, love you guys." She says coming around with a poster of us in her hand. "Can all of you please sign this for me?"

"Sure." I respond. I take the poster and pen out her outstretched hand, and I sign it.

"And since I have you standing here with me. Can you take a selfie with me?"

"Sure." I laugh.

"Thank you. Thank you. My granddaughters are going to flip when I show them your pic. They just love you."

"Well it was nice meeting you Miss..."

"You can call me Donna."

"Okay. Are you going to the show tomorrow night?"

"What kind of question is that? Of course!"

"Well I hope you enjoy the show tomorrow. If you would excuse us Miss Donna. We have an interview to do."

"Of course boys! Go on in. I'm sure Steve is ready for ya."

Everyone signs the poster, then we walk behind two double doors and into the radio station.

New York's popular DJ, Steve sits behind a control panel with a pair of sunglasses on and of course he's wearing our t-shirt. He motions us to sit around the large table and raises his hand, signaling to us to give him a minute.

"New York!" He screams into his microphone. Guess who's in the studio... You guess it! The hottest rock band around right now. Wildfire! That's right! Who wants to go to their concert tomorrow tonight? What the hell. I'll give you tickets if you're caller number ten. So hit me up. In the meantime, let's listen to their current number one single that I'm sure will be going platinum soon and it's called, Your Love." He taps a button and he removes his headset.

"Well how the fuck are you guys this afternoon?" He says with excitement in his voice.

"We're doing." Caleb responds.

"I see. You guys are blowing up the charts. Well I must say I'm happy to have you guys here. Just like any interview you've been to. I'll ask you some simple questions, I'll give some of your fans a chance to call in, and I'll see you guys on your way. Sound cool?"

We all nod our heads in acknowledgment that we understood.

"Alright well go ahead and put on your headsets and let's get started."

Steve pushes a button and we begin.

"What's up to all the Wildfire fans out there! I still need a caller number ten so I can give away these tickets, we're going to go ahead and open the phone lines for anyone out there who would like to ask Wildfire a question. And look a there. The lines are already blowing up! So Wildfire you guys are really hot right now, did you ever think you would become so big in such a little amount of time?"

"I'll answer that Steve." Caleb says bringing his mouth close to the microphone. "First I would like to say hello to all our fans. Without you we wouldn't be here right now, but to answer your question. We didn't know where our music would take us. If it wasn't for Sierra, the owner of The Grind who decided to give us a chance we probably wouldn't be sitting here right now, and of course there's our manager Rich, who couldn't be here today."

"I hear ya man." Steve responds. "So Mason. A lot of critics like to say you have a talented raw voice. What do you have to say about that?"

"Well Steve any good mention of how I sing or how my voice sounds. I take it as a great compliment. I even love to hear the bad reviews too, but seriously when I sing I put my all into it. I want our fans to feel what I'm feeling through the lyrics."

"Well if this counts any. Your voice is very unique. I must say you have your own sound going on." Steve says.

"Thanks Steve."

"Of course man. Well I'm going to go ahead and let some of your fans ask you a couple of questions. But before I do. Caleb how did it feel being on tour with your dad for two weeks before you guys signed your own tour contract? For those of you out there listening; who should know, he's Isaac Walker, the lead singer of Hurricane."

"It's been a learning experience. He's been doing this for a long time so when we have a problem he always gives us good advice. I'm glad he believed in us enough to invite us on tour."

"If anything I think it's just helping his career, but don't tell him I told you that." Steve jokes. "Okay let's take some fan calls. You're live with Steve and Wildfire. Caller go ahead with your question.

I can't believe I got through. I'm so freakin' out right now, but anyways. My question is for all of you. Are you single?"

"How did I know that question was coming?" Steve asks.

227

"I'm single." Caleb responds.

"I would rather stay single because I have a lot of love to give." Evan speaks up.

"What's up New York. This is your boy Jax. I'm very single, but if any of you ladies have the guts to approach me. Who knows what will happen."

"This is Jeremy and I'm also single."

"And that leaves you Mason." Steve says into his microphone.

"Well unlike my band mates I actually have someone very special in my life right now."

"Whoa! I'm sure you just broke a million men and women's hearts just now. So who is this special someone?"

"I respect her privacy so I won't say her name on the air, but I will say this. If she's listening right now. I want to let her know that two months without her has been pure total hell and I can't wait to have her in my arms tonight."

"So she lives in New York then?"

"She does."

"Hmm. Well ladies I'm sorry but it seems like Mason is taken. But I'm still single ladies." Steve laughs. "Well it was a pleasure meeting all of you. When you're back in the area. Please stop by."

"We will and thanks for having us." I respond. "You should come out tomorrow night. I'm sure we can get you backstage."

"Trust me. I'll be there." Steve responds. "That's all for me today folks. I would like to say congratulations to Teresa. She was our caller number ten. Don't forget to catch Wildfire tomorrow night at the Madison Square Garden. This is Steve with 108.6 Rock On, signing off."

twenty-four
Nyla

"Nyla!"

I hear someone calling my name.

I turn around and see Jordyn running after me.

"Hey." She says catching up to me. I didn't see you in Biology today. That's not like you. Are you okay?"

"Yeah. I'm good. Just feeling a little under the weather. Did I miss anything that would require me to copy your lecture notes?"

"Actually you did, but I'm sure your nerdy ass will catch on quick."

"Whatever." I say while rolling my eyes.

"So are you heading back to the apartment?"

"Yeah. I told Brooke I would show her around the city, before I see Mason tonight."

"Well I can't wait to meet your man tomorrow night. I'm heading to the mall to find something to wear to the concert."

All of a sudden I start to feel weak and sick at the same time. I stop walking and I place my right hand over my stomach.

"You okay?" Jordyn asks me.

"I'm fine. I'll see you later okay? I'm going to head to the drug store and get some stomach medicine."

"Okay girl." I hope you get to feeling better."

"Thanks."

Jordyn walks away and I continue my walk on the side walk, making a stop at the campus bookstore instead. I walk inside and I make my way past the drinks, snacks, magazines, medicines, and I stop in front of the feminine products. My eyes roam over the tampons, and the pads. Landing on the pregnancy tests.

I can't believe I'm even thinking about taking one of these. I've been on birth control since I was a teenager, because of irregular periods, and of course to prevent pregnancy, and I never missed a pill. Even though I was on the pill I made sure I had condoms. I think back to all the times when Mason and I were intimate. We didn't use condoms all the time but I was still on the pill, so why was I debating on taking a test? Being a Pre-med student I should have known better than to not use a backup method while being on antibiotics. Even the warning label on the bottle tells you that birth control can become ineffective and you can become pregnant. *How could I be so careless?* I grab two tests off the shelf. One digital and one that revealed the results by showing a plus or minus sign. I make my way to the counter to pay for my items. As soon as they are bagged, I grab them off the counter and I make my way home.

* * *

Thirty minutes later. I'm standing in my bathroom looking at both tests showing the same results. Before I could process how I was feeling about my results, I hear Brooke yelling my name from the living room.

"Nyla!" Hurry up and get in here. I walk out my bathroom and bedroom, then I rush down the hall to the living room where Brooke stood watching a gossip news television show. On the bottom of the screen, the words breaking news were scrolling across.

"What is it?" I ask her.

"Shhh. Listen." She lifts the remote and cuts the volume up.

Just hours ago we received news that Mason and Caleb, members of Wildfire are brothers. This picture was leaked to the press just minutes ago.

I gasp when I see the same picture I saw wedged in the photo album at the Walker's house, pop up on the screen.

We are unsure of who leaked the photo, but sources say that these allegations are true. Along with the picture we also received an official birth certificate that shows Isaac Walker is the father of Mason Scott. Our people have tried to get in contact with all three parties involved. Isaac and Mason have failed to comment but this is what Caleb had to say.

The screen changes and a prerecorded video of Caleb shows up.

I should be surprised but I'm not. For all I know my dad could have other children out there. I just hate this comes out now, and right before our concert. I hope this doesn't change my relationship with Mason because I've always looked at him as a brother just like the rest of my bandmates. He's the innocent one in this situation.

Then the cameraman shows Caleb walking away.

I turn to look at Brooke. "So does that mean he's your father too?"

"No!" Brooke says while shaking her head no. "Mason and I just have the same mom."

"Have you talked to Mason?" I continue.

"No he won't answer his phone." Brooke says sounding worried.

"Shit." I rush back to my room and I grab my phone. I call Mason first but it goes straight to voicemail. Next I call Caleb, and he answers on the second ring.

"Caleb. Can you text me the address to your hotel?"

twenty-five
Mason

I'm sitting at the bar in the hotel staring at what I think is my fifth tequila shot. The bartender tries to cut me off, but all I had to do was flash him a hundred dollar bill, and the drinks kept coming. I glance up at the flat screen television hanging on the wall showing breaking news clips of my new chaotic life. *Isaac Walker is my dad?* My phone vibrates against the bar's counter for the hundredth time. I pick it up and see it's Nyla again. I press the ignore button then I signal the bartender over.

"I'll have another..."

"I'll have what he's having, and you can put it on my tab." A female voice orders the bartender. I turn my head and see a pretty red head. Her eyes were green and she had lips made for sin. My eyes continue down and land on a pair of fake tits.

"See something you want?" She asks leaning into me. "How about we go back to your room and I'll make you forget about all your problems."

"Really?" I asked drunk out my mind?

"Yes really."

"I'll pass. I have someone special in my life right now, and I refuse to mess it up."

"Too bad. So where's your special someone now? As sexy as you are I wouldn't leave you at a bar drinking away your sorrows."

"I refuse to let her see me like this."

"I'm sorry to hear that. How about this. Let's go to your room and I'll suck your dick and fuck your brains out. How does that sound? It will be our little secret and your special someone will never find out. So what do you say. Wanna get out of here?"

twenty-six
Nyla

My taxi pulls up to the five-star hotel and I see nothing but reporters standing around. On my way here I called Caleb letting him know I was just around the corner, and he told me that he would be on the lookout for my taxi.

I pay the driver and I get out. I walk towards the crowded entrance, but I stop when I see someone wearing a baseball cap walking in my direction. He lifts the hat up a little so I could see his face. *Caleb.*

"Hey." He says, pulling me into a hug.

"Hey." I respond pulling away. "Is it always this crazy at every hotel you're at?"

"Sometimes, but since that story hit the media, every got damn news show and magazine column have been parked outside the hotel."

"How are we supposed to get inside?"

"Side entrance. Let's go."

I follow Caleb to the other entrance of the hotel. He swipes his card and immediately we're given entrance.

We walk in and take the elevator to the lobby floor. The elevator doors open and we step out walking around people who were going on with their daily lives. We continue to walk, making our way to the hotel bar.

"I spoke to Jeremy before you came, and he mentioned something about Mason being down here." Caleb says over his shoulder. I continue to follow him until the bar comes into view, and there sitting at the bar was Mason, and he wasn't alone.

"Shit." I could hear Caleb say. As we make our way to where he was sitting with another female.

We come to a stop right behind Mason's stool without bringing any attention to us.

"I told you I have someone." I could hear Mason slur.

"Again she's not here is she?" The bitch says while running her hand up and down his thigh. "Come on let me take..."

"Bitch are you deaf? I think he just told you that he

isn't interested." I interrupt.

Mason clumsily turns around on his stool and sees me standing there with Caleb with a look of relief on his face.

"Well it looks like you came just in time sweetheart because I was getting ready to have a lot of fun with him." She says while allowing her eyes to trace over Mason.

"Yeah. Well I guess you'll need to find someone else's man to fuck."

"Damn." Caleb says behind me.

"It's his loss. How about you?" She asks looking over my shoulder at Caleb.

"Well..."

"Caleb." I say through gritted teeth. "Help me get Mason to the room."

"Well maybe next time." The red head responds. Then she walks off.

"Come on let's get you out of here." Caleb says.

We help Mason to a standing position. We both wrap

one of his arms around our neck. Mason turns his head in my direction and says my name. The smell of tequila on his breath has me feeling nauseous. I turn my head away to take several deep breathes.

"Nyla you ready?" Caleb asks me.

I turn to Caleb and I can see the look of concern on his face.

"Yes." I finally respond.

We make our way pass the lobby where you could see through the automatic doors, a swarm of reporters and paparazzi trying to get in, but security was preventing that.

We step into the elevator, Caleb swipes his keycard and we make our way up to their penthouse suite.

I unwrap Mason's arm from around my neck and I allow him to put all his weight on Caleb, then I move to stand on the other side of Caleb, waiting on the elevator to stop.

"Nyla." Mason slurs my name again. He takes his arm from around Caleb, and tries standing on his own but stumbles back. "I wasn't going to fuck her." He continues.

"Man if I were you. I would shut the fuck up right now." Caleb suggests.

"Baby are you listening to me?" Mason slurs again.

I ignore him, and I continue to wait. The elevator eventually comes to a stop.

"Where's your key and which penthouse are you guys in?" I direct my question to Caleb.

After he tells me the room information, he gives me his key. The elevator doors open and I leave Caleb and Mason behind. I make my way down the hall to their suite. I insert the key and as soon as I have the door open, I rush inside.

I keep straight, walking past the kitchen where I see Jeremy.

"What's up Nyla. You alright?" He asks me.

"Where's the bathroom?" I ask him.

"Down the hall to your left."

I jog down the hall, and into the bathroom slamming the door behind me. I drop to my knees in front of the toilet and I release all the contents in my stomach up. Once I'm done, I flush the toilet and I go to the sink to wash my hands, and I rinse my mouth out with the hotel's complimentary mouth wash. I take a seat on the edge of the huge bath tub and I break down. Unable to keep the tears from falling.

A light knock on the door has me wiping away my tears quickly.

"Who is it?"

"It's Caleb."

"Come in."

He sticks his head in and I wave him in.

"Close the door." I say to him.

"Are you crying?"

"Where's Mason?" I ask him. Ignoring his question.

"In his room. Knocked out."

"Okay good."

"Are you going to explain to me why you're crying?"

I look up into his eyes and the tears start falling again.

"Shit Nyla. What's wrong? Don't let what happened at the bar get to you."

"It's not that."

"Okay. Then what is it. Talk to me. You've got me worried over here."

After sitting there for several moments, trying to get my nerves in check. I look back up at Caleb. "I'm pregnant." I respond with tears running down my face.

"Nyla." He says my name in a calming voice. "Come here." I stand and I walk into his open arms.

"Everything is going to be okay." He whispers to me. "Have you told anyone else?"

"No you're the first to know. If Mason wasn't drunk right now, I would tell him."

"How long have you known?"

"I found out today. I took two tests and they both came out positive. What is Mason going to think? Everything is happening so fast."

"Shhh. I'm sure everything will be okay. Just talk to him, and if he decides he doesn't want you or the baby to be a part of his life, just know I'm always here for you."

"Thanks Caleb."

"Any time big head."

We both laugh while still embracing each other.

"How are you holding up?" I ask him.

"I'm fine. There's so much you don't know, but I'll be okay. I really hate it for Mason though."

"Have you talked to him or your parents?"

"Mason? No not yet, and I'm just not ready to face my parents right now."

"Well if you need to talk to someone, I'm here for you."

"I appreciate that Nyla."

He kisses the top of my head and pulls away.

"You look tired." Caleb says, looking down at me.

"I am."

"Come on. I'll let you have my room and I'll take the couch."

Too tired to argue. I agree.

He hugs me to his body and walks me out the bathroom and across the hall to his room.

"If you need me, I'll be in the living room. Good night."

"Good night Caleb."

He closes the door behind him leaving me alone. I was so exhausted and hungry since I haven't been able to keep anything down lately.

"Bath. Snack. Bed." I say to myself.

I walk into the bathroom and I run a warm bath. After several minutes of bathing and soaking in the tub. I dry myself off, and I wrap a towel around my body. I walk out the bathroom yawning several times.

Snack later. Sleep now.

I pull back the covers, leaving the towel wrapped around me, and I get in. I pull the covers up to my shoulders and as soon as my head hits the feather stuffed pillow, I was fast asleep.

twenty-seven
Mason

After a long hot shower. I still felt like shit. My head was pounding and I needed to get some food in my stomach. I make my way into the kitchen, but pause when I see Caleb sitting at the table drinking a cup of coffee and reading the newspaper.

"Morning."

He looks up and acknowledges my presence.

"Morning. How are you feeling?"

"Like shit. Man I'm trying to piece together what happened last night. I don't remember falling asleep. All I remember is going down to the bar, I briefly remember some girl with fake boobs trying to get me to fuck her and everything after that I have no clue."

"Sounds like you got real fucked up man." Caleb says then pauses for a moment. "How much do you care about Nyla?" He continues.

"What kind of question is that? You know I would do anything for her."

"Really?"

"Yes!"

Caleb stands up and walks over to where I'm standing and leans against the counter. "Nyla is like a little sister to me. I know things are crazy right now especially since we just found out that we're brothers. We're blood. But let me tell you this. If you hurt Nyla in any way I'm going to fuck you up."

"What? Look Caleb I know you and Nyla have been friends for a long time and you care about her. Just know..."

"Just know what? That you'll never hurt her?"

"Man what's your fuckin' point?"

"My point is instead of you going to the bar to drink away your problems you should have been with her. Do you remember how you got back to your room? Oh wait I forgot. You were too drunk! You should have saw the look on Nyla's face when she saw you sitting at the bar with that bitch hanging all over you. When we walked over to get you, I thought she was going to beat the shit out of you, but then we overheard you telling her that you weren't interested. Man we helped your ass last night! But of course you can't remember."

Caleb pushes off the counter getting ready to exit the kitchen but stops. "Get your shit together man. You're not the only one going through something right now. Oh and by the way. Nyla wasn't feeling so well last night so I told her to crash here. She's asleep in my room if you wanted to know." Then he leaves the kitchen, making me feel worse than I did before. If that was possible.

twenty-eight
Nyla

The warm touch of someone's hand rubbing gentle circles against my naked stomach awakens me. I open my eyes and see Mason looking down at me.

"Good morning. Caleb told me that you got sick last night. How are you feeling?"

"Better now. I'm actually pretty hungry."

"Do you want me to fix you something to eat?"

"Toast. Nothing too heavy, and a glass of orange juice if you have any."

"Anything else?"

"No. I think that will do."

"Are you sure? With you eating for two now. Do you think that will be enough?"

All I could do was stare at him speechless.

He reaches over me and grabs my cellphone off the nightstand. "Your phone has been going off all morning, so I thought I would turn it off for you, so you could get your rest but I didn't because of I saw this."

He turns the phone so I could see the screen.

Jordyn: Nyla are you PREGO? I found two pregnancy tests in your bathroom and they don't belong to me or Brooke. Call me ASAP.

I read the words over and over not believing this was actually happening. Tears start to well up in my eyes.

"Mason."

"Is it true?" He asks me.

"Yes." I choke out.

"So we're having a baby?"

I nod my head yes trying to gage his reaction. "This wasn't supposed to happen this way. I should have been more careful. When I got sick, the antibiotics I was on prevented my birth control from working properly. I wasn't thinking. I'm a Pre-Med student and I should know better."

"Maybe it was meant to be. This may shock you, but this is probably the best news I've received in a while."

"Really? Because I'm scared out my mind."

Mason lowers his head and places a kiss to my lips.

"Nyla look at me."

I look up into his eyes and he wipes away the tears from my face. "We did this together. Stop putting all the blame on yourself."

"Well trust me when I tell you that I didn't mean for you to find out this way."

"How did you find out?"

"Well I've been feeling nauseous lately. I was thinking that maybe it was due to me not eating right. I've been busy and eating snacks on the go because of my school schedule. Then two nights ago Jordyn asked me if I had any tampons. It then dawned on me that I hadn't gotten my period. So yesterday I bought two tests and they both came back positive."

"So what happens next?"

"I'll call my doctor's office Monday and schedule an appointment."

"Let me know when your appointment is so I can try to be there."

"Okay I will."

We laid there in silence, letting the fact that we were going to be parents sink in.

"Nyla. About last night."

"We don't have to talk about it right now. You've been through so much already."

"Thank you." He responds before leaning in to kiss my lips again.

twenty-nine
Mason

"New York!" I scream into the microphone.

The fans in the arena go wild.

"I hope you enjoyed the show tonight, but of course all things must come to an end."

Wildfire. Wildfire. Wildfire. The fans begin to chant.

I motion to the stage hands and they bring out a stool and my guitar.

"How many of you out there have ever been in love?" I ask the crowd. I grab my guitar and take a seat on the stool. I adjust the microphone, then I pull out my earpiece.

We love you Mason!

"I love you too. But seriously. How many of you have found that one person that you would do anything for, and you feel that life isn't worth living unless you have them there with you?"

The fans continue to scream.

"Well I have a confession... I have. Matter of fact do you want to meet her?" I turn my head to the left and see Nyla standing there with Brooke and Jordyn, shaking her head no with a look of horror on her face.

"Baby do you want to come out and meet our fans?"

Brooke was trying to push her on stage, but she kept refusing.

"I think she's a bit shy. Too bad because I really wanted everyone to meet the special lady in my life. "

Awww. Some fans responded.

I'll be your girl! Others shouted.

"While on tour I wrote a song about her. It only took me a day to write it. With a little help from my brother Caleb. I was able to turn it into a masterpiece. Do you guys want to hear it?"

Yes!

"Baby this is for you. The name of this song is called Number One Fan."

The crowd settles down, patiently waiting.

I close my eyes and my guitar pick moves across the strings, creating a calm but beautiful melody. I part my lips and I let my heart do the singing. My song was about her, so it wasn't too hard for my emotions to get involved. I wanted her to know how I felt about her. How much I needed her. Adored her. How bad I wanted her to remain mine and only mine.

I pause and I stand to remove my guitar strap from around my neck, letting my band mates to continue on with the melody of my song. I grab the microphone and I break down. Pouring my soul out with every lyric that came flowing from my mouth.

I turn my attention to the one who inspired me to write the song, just to see her face streaked with tears, but nonetheless, she had a smile on her face.

* * *

"So what are we getting into tonight? The night is still young. I say we hit the town and see what Manhattan has to offer us." Jax offers, while we make our way to the end of the hall to get to the private exit of the arena.

"You guys go ahead and enjoy yourselves. I thing Nyla and I are going to stay in tonight."

"Man there's no telling when you'll be able to come back to New York. Let's enjoy this night. We'll be leaving in two days to head to Las Vegas." Evans says.

"True but I know I'll be back. Plus, Nyla and I have a lot to catch up on."

"Well while you two quote catch up. Jordyn and Brooke, you're more than welcome to chill with us tonight." Caleb suggests.

"Cool. Maybe I can show you guys around our city. Take you to some of the hot spots." Jordyn responds.

"Fine let's do it." Caleb shouts.

We push our way through the double doors of the exit and into the cool night air, where our transportation waited.

"You two enjoy your night. I know we will." Jeremy says before getting into an oversized black SUV, with everyone following behind him. Evan was the last to get in. As soon as he shuts the door, the SUV pulls away, and into the busy Manhattan nightlife.

"Ready babe?"

"Very."

I slide my fingers through hers, interlocking our hands together, and I guide her to our waiting vehicle. Our driver opens the door and we get in. When the door closes beside me I pull Nyla into my arms. The driver gets in and drives us to her apartment.

thirty
Nyla

"I didn't stay here last night so if my apartment is a mess. Blame it on Jordyn and Brooke."

"Baby just open the door." He whispers against my neck. "Do you know how long I've patiently waited to have you to myself? I wanted to make love to you this morning, but since we were in Caleb's bed, and I have a lot of respect for him I didn't. Now open the door."

I insert my key into the door, and he pushes it open. We step inside and he closes the door and locks it behind us. I turn my attention to Mason, giving him an innocent look.

"Can I get you something to eat or drink?"

"No I'm good babe."

"Okay. I'm going to get a quick snack and after that we can chill on the couch and watch some tv."

I walk into the kitchen and I open the pantry and pull out some microwave popcorn. I tear it open and I place it into the microwave to cook. I turn around and see Mason leaning against the wall looking at me.

"Want me to show you around?" I ask him.

"Maybe tomorrow." He steps away from the wall and comes to stand in front of me. "How about you show me what's underneath this tight ass black dress." His hands linger at the hem of my dress. Just the slight touch of his fingertips brushing against my thighs was sending chills throughout my body, and straight to the spot between my legs.

"This old thing?" I ask breathless. Looking into his eyes, still keeping my innocent act. "There's nothing under this dress that I think you'll find interesting."

"Try me."

Damn he always knew how to make me feel so sexy. I hope he continues to months from now when my stomach starts growing and other body parts start changing. Will he feel the same?

I reach up and release my hair from its bun and I let my hair fall past my shoulders. I turn around and I lift my hair up, before looking over my shoulder at him. "Do you think you can help me with my zipper?"

His hands slide up my body and he slowly pulls my zipper down.

I turn around and I pull the sleeves off my shoulders and I allow the dress to slide to the floor. Then I step out of my pumps and I walk around Mason, giving him a view of my naked body.

"Are you going to just stand there remembering how it feels to be inside me? Or do you want to find out?" I walk out the kitchen and I make my way to my bedroom. Looking over my shoulder once, to see Mason following behind me.

I walk into my room and I crawl to the middle of my bed and I turn around to see Mason walking in. He stands at the foot of my bed and removes his clothes and shoes. "Open your legs." He tells me and I comply. He crawls up my bed to me, and rests his hips between my legs. He lowers his head and kisses my forehead. "I missed you." He confesses then he kisses both of my cheeks, the tip of my nose, lips, chin, between my breasts, and down to my belly button where he gently touches my stomach.

"I'm going to get so big."

"Only because you're carrying our baby." He says while placing tender kisses against my flat stomach. "I can't wait to see how big you'll get."

"Will you think I'm still sexy?" I ask, looking down at him.

"Baby you'll always be sexy to me. Do you wanna know what I think is really sexy?"

"Tell me."

"The way you look and sound when you're coming, and especially when you're calling out my name."

He starts kissing his way back up my body.

"Mmm Mason." I moan.

"Yes. Just like that."

"He continues his kisses up, finally coming face to face with me. Staring into my eyes I could see he had something he wanted to say.

"What is it?" I ask him while running my hands through his hair.

He lowers his head and kisses my lips and reaches between my legs and inserts two fingers inside of me. Never answering my question.

"Are you ready for me?" He asks me.

"You know I am."

He removes his fingers and places the tip of his dick at my entrance, and enters me. "I swear your pussy was made for me. You wrap around me so perfectly."

"Yes." A breathless moan slips from my lips. I spread my legs a little wider and I relax my muscles.

Mason pushes his hips forward going much deeper, filling me completely. Moving himself in and out of me while moaning out his pleasure.

"Baby I don't think I'm going to last long." He says in a strained voice.

"Me either."

We move in unison, changing our position and putting me on top of him.

He grips my hips tight and slides me up and down his length. Throwing my head back, I scream his name out in pleasure. He comes to a sitting position and I run my hands through his hair. Grabbing his silky strands, I bring his mouth to mine and I continue to work my body up and down his. Urgently seeking my release. His fingers dig into the skin on my hips, and he pushes me down hard on his length, and I scream out my release. My arms wrap lazily around his neck and the next moment I'm back on my back again.

"Stay with me Nyla. I'm so close sweetheart." He slides his arm under my lower back, lifting my ass off the bed. He circles his hips moving his length deeper inside me, while staring down into my eyes. He continues a steady rhythm of Slow. Fast. Fast. Slow. Fast. Fast. Slow. Thrusting and rotating his hips, and giving both of our bodies the pleasure it's been seeking. Several pumps later he closes his eyes and screams out my name, releasing all his built up tension inside of me. He lowers his head to the pillow and slows his pace to a stopping point. He lays on top of me, while putting all of his weight on me.

"Just give me a minute." He says into my ear, sounding exhausted.

"You're fine." I turn my head just enough to be able to kiss his lips.

"I love you." He whispers against my lips.

"I love you too." I whisper back before closing my

eyes.

Several minutes of silence pass between us to a point that I thought he had fallen asleep until I open mine to see a pair of gray ones looking at me adoringly.

"I meant what I said Nyla." He says running his thumb over my lips, then he leans in and swipes his tongue along them before gently sucking each lip at a time into his mouth, before pulling away. "You keep me going. I want to be a better person because of you. After my ma died, I pushed you away and you were so patient with me, and you never gave up on me. I don't know why you came into my life but I'm glad you did because you give me so much hope. I'm not perfect Nyla but I promise to try and be the best man and father to our baby. I am not like my father. I refuse to be. Just keep believing in me."

He kisses me again, long and hard. Mason's hips shift between my legs, and I could feel his growing erection that was still inside of me. "Tell me that you love me Nyla."

"I love you so much Mason."

For the rest of the night we reacquainted ourselves with each other's bodies. Just like Mason said earlier. We needed to catch up, and we did by making love all night until our bodies became too exhausted to function any more.

* * *

Boom. Boom. Boom.

My eyes fly open to the sound of someone banging on my front door. I sit up slowly in bed and I gather my sheet and wrap it around my body, then I slide out of bed.

"What time is?" Mason asks me. He reaches for my comforter and covers his naked body.

I tear my eyes away from him and glance at my alarm clock. "It's 8:15 am."

"Who would be knocking this early? Let whoever it is keep knocking and come back to bed babe."

"What if it's your sister and Jordyn? I don't remember hearing them come in last night, and if I remember correctly, you put the chain on the door, so they probably can't get in."

"Shit. Go see and hurry back to bed." He mumbles.

I walk out of my room and down the hall.

Boom. Boom. Boom.

"I'm coming!" I shout. I grab a hold to the sheet that was dragging around my feet and I jog the rest of the way to the door.

I undo the chain and unlock the dead bolt. I swing the door open, and I am shocked to see who's standing on the other side.

"Mom and dad?" I ask tightening the sheet around my body. "What are you doing here?" My voice was filled with shock and confusion.

"It's nice to see you too sweetheart." My mom says walking past me and into my apartment with my dad following behind her. "Can we not surprise our daughter?" She continues.

You never have before.

"We wanted to stop in and see how you were doing. Your father and I are on our way to D.C." My mom pauses and studies me. "Are you just now getting out of bed?" She asks me.

"I had a late night. Mom and dad I'm happy you stopped, but why didn't you call and tell me that you were going to be in town?"

My mom stands there looking at me real hard. Examining me like I was one of her patients. Her eyes travel up and down my body, noticing my state of dress.

"Babe are you coming back to bed?"

I turn around and see Mason standing there with nothing on except my comforter that was wrapped around his waist.

Shit.

My dad clears his throat and he takes his gaze off of Mason. "Nyla who is this young man?"

* * * To Be Continued * * *

About The Author

Hi, I'm Danyell A. Wallace. I was born in Anchorage, Alaska and I'm currently living in Alabama. I'm a mom to two awesome kids, and a wife to an incredibly busy hubby. I have an overactive imagination and I love to read, so I decided to write my own stories and books. I find that reading and writing soothes me especially when there's so much going on in this world today.

When I'm not writing, I'm spending time with my family and friends, catching up on tv shows that I have saved on my DVR, or I'm enjoying a good high school or college football game.

CPSIA information can be obtained at www.ICGtesting.com
Printed in the USA
LVOW11s1300100116

469981LV00007B/824/P